Tales for the Trail

*Flee as a bird
to your mountain*

Psalms 11:1

Tales for the Trail

stories & poems by

Boone ● Cranston ● Ford ● Groome
Gustafson ● Jauss ● King ● Mallinson
Mortenson ● Napolin ● Noyes ● Rich
Smith ● Smits ● Uncle River ● Williams

BIRCH BROOK PRESS

Compilation & Afterword:
Copyright © 2003 by Birch Brook Press

First Edition

Library of Congress Catalog Control No.: 2003106588
ISBN: 0-913559-85-7

Art by Frank C. Eckmair

This Letterpress Edition was typeset & printed at

Birch Brook Press
PO Box 81
Delhi NY 13753

Write or e-mail for free catalog of books & art
birchbrkpr@catskill.net
Visit us at www.birchbrookpress.info

Acknowledgments

"A Bear Incident" by Uncle River first appeared in *Iconoclast*, published by Philip Wagner. A slightly shortened version appears in this book.
"The Hardest Season" by Tom Noyes, from his book, *Behold Faith and Other Stories*, courtesy of Dufour Editions, Chester Springs, PA 19425. A shortened version of the story appears here.
"Climbing Down Dix Mountain" by Pamela Cranston appeared in the on-line publication, *The Adirondack Review*.

Contents

Tales for the Trail

Sequel

By Sid Gustafson

HENSON'S DEAD. I'm having trouble coming to grips with his passing. He's up here somewhere. The mist I'm flying his plane through comes and goes. Now it stays. Suddenly the cocoon of clouds opens to a carapace of earth that dashes toward me. I pull up, skimming over the back wall of death, passing close enough to kiss the top of the world. I hang on to flight and ride a Chinook wind down the east slope of the cordillera.

Darkness envelops the volatile atmosphere as I drop below the continental divide. All kinds of weather. Montana weather. This morning it was snow when I took off in a clearing of clouds. And now rain, coming and going, mostly coming. Wind of all sorts. I have some light to the west. Clouds bleed up the setting sun, an aura for Henson's repose. A grizzly bear ate him. Yeah, my close friend. Dead. Dead, and I'm not yet in touch with his departure. A part of me is perished with him, a big twisted part of me. It's quite a story, quite a life. I'm much too blear-stricken to recount it all right now, but I wrote it all down. The words are in the cockpit here, somewhere. It's been a rugged week and I have my hands full with this crippled plane. That, and now I'm into even wetter weather. Rain beats down, blinding rain that spiders across my windshield. Rivulets that distort,

waves that blur. I'm trying to make it back to his ranch
to tell his mother—his mother and children. And wife,
ex-wife. I need to land. Soon. I'm pretty sure I'm above
his ranch. The weather breaks, but not for long.

We led risky lives and his luck just plain ran out. He
wouldn't view it as bad luck though. He's an Indian, a
truly native American. Luck doesn't really have anything
to do with life, or death. Not in his view, which by now
must be omniscient.

It's tough to locate down below. My loss of luck may
not be far behind my partner's. Shearing squalls. Wind-
driven dankness. Foul weather. A pilot's nightmare.
Splattering, eyeless. Sheets and runnels. My fuel is low.
I have skis on the plane, jerry-rigged skis on a broken
landing gear (another story I'm too preoccupied to re-
late). Well, at least I had skis when I took off. I topped
some trees on the way up out of the river bottom. I think
I might have tore off the right set, snow skis Henson and
I carefully strapped and riveted on to the landing gear he
bent when we were forced to land on a river bank well
over a week ago. And then there was the blizzard, snow
and cold, bitter, and now rain.

At last I make out the faint silhouette of prairie be-
low, a dusky dimming windswept expanse. The rain
blows away. Relief. Scant relief. No lights in sight. A
contourless earth. No snow for a smooth landing. Black-
feet Indian Reservation nothingness. Henson's ancestral
homeland. I imagine the thick clumps of native bunch-
grass, nothing quite as soft as snow. The wind sweeps me
down the fall of mountains. I let it take me eastward and

when I'm far enough out I nose back around into the Chinook blow. I lose altitude, careening with the wind, until I spot the vague elevation of a hogback ridge running out of the Rocky Mountain Front. I line up and bring my craft earthbound hoping not to auger in. I stuff some blankets and a pillow in front of my chest and check my seat belt, tightening it as snug as I can. Could be rough coming in for this one.

Below all I can make out are shades of purple. And wind, wicked wind. I heave my craft against her howling. I nose straight into her and hold tight. I ease down a bit closer. Pretty tricky flying, I'll tell ya. The darkening world rises toward me. I'm almost stationary to the ground flying into this fierce wind. This may be good. Landspeed nearly nil. My headwind a Godsend. I've brought a lot of crippled planes down in my time, but this takes the cake. Wind, skis (half a set and a deplorable lack of snow), no airfield, no runway lights. No instruments, no radar. This ain't Vietnam. And I ain't so young and cocky anymore. Scared, scared and old. That's me in this precarious spiral.

Darkness deepens. My flight thins. New spirits of rain break across my windshield and spider my view. Earth mesmerizes me. My ground speed stops, slows, then surges sidelong. There are moments I'm blown backwards. I pitch and yaw, yaw and dip, dip and dive. The deranged wind makes it so. I pray. Pilots do pray, you know. Jesus do we pray. A brief smoothness in the flow descends upon me. Everything shifts to slo-mo and I drop in on a nimble ridge of grass when I have half a

chance. I touch the left landing gear's skis to the grass.
They grab and hop, grab and hop. Whoa. I reef on the
flaps, get the tail down, the right landing gear dips and
spikes its skiless gaff into the earth and my world
tumbles. I cartwheel. Slowly at first, then everything
reels akimbo—off I roll into a feigning crepuscule of
twilight. . . .

I awaken to darkness. Blood and darkness and fuel drip-
ping. Mind whirling. A gash of midnight suffused in a
gassed upsidedownness. My mouth bleeds. I spit out
teeth. I taste the ferric promise of life. I smell the ethe-
real curse of death. Too late for an explosion, probably.
My head throbs. My ear aches. I touch it and feel an
eerie splay of cartilage. My fingers come back bloody. I
dither. Spin. I am spinning, earthbound spinning.
    I wait.
    The flying rule is: When in doubt, do nothing. But
I'm not flying anymore. I think I'm not.
    The wind blows. The plane creaks and whistles,
nudging shrill in its crumpled angle of repose. Oh, my.
My oh my. I finally decide to unstrap. Click—I crumple
to the ceiling. I wrestle up the door and wind fills the
fuselage, turbocharging me with breath. I struggle into
the night. Once outside I'm blown away from the plane.
My face stings. My muscles twitch. My bones bend,
muscles twang. I hug the earth. The Chinook wind is
warm, almost hot, but it is not the wind so much as my
twisted fate that heats me. I curl into the soft bunchgrass
fescue. Fetally grounded, my body quivers in aftershock.

12

SEQUEL

I wait, wait for the sun to light my newfound world.
Or maybe the moon. And in my wait I sleep. And in this
coma I dream vacuous dreams, their memory shucked
away by the howl of the Chinook wind, until a dream
comes along that I can hold onto. A dream of cleanliness.
A dream of bathing. With a woman. I cannot hold the
dream in place, so I pocket the memory and roll to my
back and gaze upward, the labyrinthian gauze of stars
enraptures me. A clock in my heart. A fleecing Milky
Way spills its infinity across the silver pepper of a be-
smirched firmament.

I let the darkness of night mingle with the darkness
of my soul.

And the darkness is not perfect, but neither is my
soul. I know also that the darkness is not permanent, and
now I know that neither is the darkness that once en-
gulfed my soul.

Under the scrutiny of stars I bear the black weight
of my melancholy. Out of the deepest cavern of night a
calloused moon makes its way into the starblown sky.
A calloused and waning gibbous moon. Blood-red as it
rises from the horizon, leviathan of eternity. Membran-
ous as it clears the earth. Its light is not perfect or per-
manent, but its company caresses me to sleep. Sleep in
which I dream in a halo of happiness—perhaps a concus-
sion—and dream some more. I am finally getting in
touch with my dreams. I am 10, maybe 12 days without
alcohol, and that after 10, maybe 12, years with, perpetu-
ally cottoned against the pain of living. And despite the
wrecked plane, my wrecked life, my dead flying mate,

and the imperfect but impermanent darkness of my soul,
I have a new outlook. I can't tell you why—not here and
now—you'll have to read the book that is crinkled and
wadded in the plane, the book I wrote in the wilderness,
the wilderness that just spit me out of its scrupulous
paradise.

Canoeing at Dawn
On the Chippewa River

Each stroke of my paddle
raises a scallop of white.

Up ahead, a northern pike
jumps. Its green scales
flash red-gold.

Nearby, a deer
vanishes into the poplars,
its white tail bobbing
like a feather
in an Ojibwa headdress.

And as I round the bend
I shed centuries like old skin.
Only moments ago
I rose from the steaming mud in a daze

and shook my wet fur.

—*David Jauss*

No Trails to Follow

By Harry Groome

GOAL-ORIENTED was the way I saw it. Nothing
more.

In a small clearing by the trailhead I worked my
arms through the padded straps of my backpack and
hunched its thirty-eight pounds in place on my shoulders
and hips. *It's not like I'm the only person who's ever tried to
do it*, I thought. *Almost forty-two hundred have gone before
me. Why is she making such a fuss?*

I unlatched the cover to a desk-like structure painted
chocolate brown with the bright yellow letters, PLEASE
REGISTER. IT'S FOR YOUR PROTECTION AND
FOR OUR INFORMATION, and wrote in the dog-eared
register: June 23, 1998. Bret Miller. Saratoga Springs
NY. Length of Stay: Three days. Planned Route: Mt.
Seymour and the Seward range via Ward Brook.

I ran my finger up several pages until it settled on
the name I was looking for, Henri Vanier. I tapped
Vanier's name twice, shook my head and smiled, and
flipped the register closed and latched the door shut.
"He's a machine," I said.

I felt strong as I started to hike. The morning was
cool, the sun still low, and my bald head was shaded by
the trees that surrounded the trail. I thought it was a
comfortable beginning and tried to calculate how many
trees were in the Adirondacks. *Six billion, a thousand for*

each acre that makes up the park? Not nearly enough. Six trillion? A quadrillion? I thought only a mathematician like me could fathom the concept of a quadrillion—fifteen zeroes are just too many for most people to comprehend, so I settled on ten trillion.

Who cares, anyway? Certainly not Melanie. She thinks I overdo my interest in numbers, my desire to be precise. She calls it anal. I tell her I just want to get things right.

I leapt from rock to rock, log to log, and crossed a network of small brooks that cut their way through the trail and skirted the black mud that waited in low pockets to inhale my hiking boots, frequently wiping myself clean of spider webs that clung to my legs and hands. Sweat darkened my green tee shirt as I began my attempt to finish climbing all the mountains over four thousand feet in the Adirondacks. If all went as planned, I'd climb my forty-third mountain today and tomorrow I'd reach the summits of numbers forty-four, forty-five and, finally, forty-six.

My pursuit hadn't begun much differently from many of my others; it just developed. It began one September when my wife Melanie had suggested we spend a weekend hiking in the Adirondacks. "It'll be beautiful with the autumn colors," she had said. "Lots of exercise and fresh mountain air. Something relaxed and fun for a change." It was typical of Melanie, prodding me to put enjoyment first.

In a little over an hour I'd covered two miles and estimated it would take another two hours and thirty minutes to cover the remaining two-point-eight miles to the shelter at Ward Brook. I could be precise about that, but as my adventure wore on the number of things I could be certain of would diminish, for the mountains I'd be climbing didn't have any trails. Instead, I'd be following stream beds and herd paths, paths made by other climbers as they tried to navigate their way to the summits, many leading nowhere as their creators had started off in the wrong direction, then backtracked, leaving a maze of dead-end choices. In turn, I'd be reading helpful signs left by those who had gone before me to mark where to cross a stream, follow a herd path, turn a new direction, change my course.

Shortly I reached a clearing where, on one side of the trail, all the trees were dead for hundreds of yards, gray and jagged in the still, dark water that surrounded them. I worked my way out of my pack and took my first drink of water. I studied the black water to the north, then my map. Blueberry Pond. Eager to finish what I'd set out to do, I decided not to stop again until I reached the Ward Brook lean-to. When I'd told Melanie about my plan to climb all forty- six, four years before on the summit of Whiteface Mountain, she'd called it obsessive.

"Obsessive?" I'd said. "It sounds like fun."

She looked at me, squinting and shading her eyes. "It sounds like *your* idea of fun."

"What's that mean?" I said.

"You take everything in life that's enjoyable and set a goal for it," she told me. "Now it's climbing mountains. Hiking was supposed to be fun, for both of us, not another obsession of yours." She'd ended by saying, "Please, Bret, don't ruin this, too."

I arrived at the lean-to at exactly eleven-thirty. The open-fronted log structure sat in a small clearing in the woods, north of the trail. On the roof, a dark sign with yellow lettering confirmed I was at Ward Brook. In front of the shelter stood a stone fireplace, a wooden table and benches. I wondered if Vanier slept here or in the mountains.

Claiming part of the lean-to by rolling out my sleeping bag and stashing my heavy pack in a far corner of the shelter, I then organized my daypack for the afternoon's climb. By twelve forty-five I was ready to begin and read the notes I'd stapled to my map: Seymour—follow brook SE. of lean-to until you reach a slide that leads to ridge—follow ridge to summit. Compass reading from entrance of brook to summit: 174°. *Almost due south. The vertical ascent's not much more than 2,000 feet. On the summit by four-fifteen, back at the lean-to well before dark. A piece of cake.*

Within an hour I was sweating hard. The temperature was close to ninety with no breeze in the dense woods. At times the herd path was no wider than my shoulders, and the trees crowded me, making for slow, muggy going. I stopped for water every forty minutes, the time I'd calculated it took to hike a mile. Once I reached Seymour's steep rockslide, I was stopping frequently to catch my breath and to let my heart quiet its pounding. The climb became steeper as I traversed the ridge. By three forty-five the altimeter on my watch read 4,000 feet and I knew I must be near the summit, although I couldn't see anything but thick growths of spruces and firs that covered the top of the mountain.

I took one last break before pushing on, drinking in large gulps, letting water run down my beard to my neck to cool me. My green shirt and shorts clung to me, dark and heavy with sweat, and black mud streaked down my short, heavy legs, caking at the tops of my socks. I was a mess and wondered how Melanie stayed so clean when she climbed. I thought of her long-limbed strength, and the small sweat patterns she always apologized for. But I liked her sweat. I liked what it said about her, what it said about us. And, in those special moments, it tasted right. *How could my wanting to climb these mountains ruin that?*

At twelve minutes past four I reached the summit. It was marked by a metal canister hanging from a large balsam tree with SEYMOUR 4,120 painted on it in faded blue letters. I slid my pack off, drew the climber's log from the canister and found a spot to rest in the stunted trees that surrounded me. I smiled as I wrote: "June 23, 1998. Bret Miller. Saratoga Springs NY. Only three more to go!" On the border of my map I wrote the names of the last three climbers to reach the summit before me, proof that I'd climbed each mountain.

My work done, I drank more water, ate a pack of peanut butter crackers and studied a narrow view of the Seward range, the tree-covered mountains I would climb the next day. I thumbed back through the log in search of Vanier, the climber whose entries I'd first noticed the summer before. I didn't have to look far. He'd signed in on June 19: Henri Vanier. Montreal. #3,885W. "The ultimate climber," I said. The sound of my voice was out of place but comforting. It made me feel less alone.

I continued my search through the log. Vanier had signed in on May 8, April 11, and March 2. He'd climbed the forty-six peaks during the winter months to earn the W after his number, and now, as if that wasn't challenge enough, he was trying to climb all the major peaks in every month of the year. *And Melanie thinks* I'm *obsessive? Does Vanier have a wife—a Melanie—in his life?* I wondered. *How does* she *react to his goal-setting?*

But I couldn't help but think that if all went well tomorrow, maybe becoming a winter climber might be next for me, too.

I arrived back at Ward Brook at seven-ten, pleased to be ahead of schedule. Two sleeping bags were rolled out on the other side of the lean-to from mine. I was glad to have other climbers to share my experiences with, and for a moment hoped that one of them was Melanie; that she'd hiked in to surprise me.

I collected a dry tee shirt and shorts, my water purifier, water bottles and a small towel and walked to the brook to the east of the lean-to. Ten yards before the brook the trees opened, giving me a clear view of the water. A young man and woman stood naked at the edge of the brook. The man's feet were in the water, his head buried between the woman's breasts. She stood on a rock and moved her body up and down on him, the muscles in her calves and thighs flexing with each move, her buttocks rotating slowly. As I turned away, the young man caught sight of me. I heard him curse, then plead with the woman not to stop. I heard her laugh.

As I walked to the next brook that crossed the trail, I became angry with Melanie, angry with myself. *How did we let things go this far? Let things get so out of control?* I pulled off my boots and sweat-soaked socks, stripped off my tee shirt and shorts and waded into the brook. I stood naked in the water and imagined for a moment that I was with Melanie, my bearded face between her breasts, making love, enjoying each other, hearing her laughter.

The young couple was cooking supper when I returned to the lean-to. I guessed they were in their late twenties. They were the same height, like Melanie and me. He was dark and strong-looking. She had long, straight blond hair and wore round, wire-rimmed glasses. The man looked at me and looked away. The woman smiled and said hello. "I'm Katie." She put out her hand. *Warm, self-assured. Melanie ten years ago.* It was that same directness—that openness—that had attracted me to her.

"Bret," I said.

Katie patted the young man's shoulder. "This is my friend Michael." We shook hands.

They were from New York City and didn't plan to do any climbing. I told them why I was there. "We're not nearly that ambitious," Katie said with a smile. "We come up here to get away from the city and have time

23

alone together. Michael and I love the woods and camp-
ing out." When she spoke I could hear Melanie's words,
"something relaxed and fun for a change," and wondered
what I was missing.

I boiled water in an aluminum pot over a small gas
stove and cooked spaghetti and clam sauce, and ate a half
bag of cookies and drank a bottle of water before my
hunger was satisfied. With an hour's more light left in the
day, I began to prepare for sleep, knowing I'd be under-
way the next morning by six. Katie and Michael walked
down the trail hand in hand as I stretched my tired legs
into my sleeping bag and zipped it about me. I imagined
them back at the brook, naked and laughing, and again
wished Melanie was with me. A feeling of regret came
over me and I felt myself flush. As I began to wind down
and give in to sleep, I wondered how I could have done
things differently.

At five the next morning I was awakened by a gray
dawn. I ate breakfast, broke camp quietly, and took one
last look at Katie, burrowed in her sleeping bag, the out-
line of her hip and shoulder and the back of her blond
head visible to me. *They're so alike*, I thought, then forced
myself to review the task that lay ahead. *Over Seward,
over Donaldson to Mount Emmons, and back. Nine to eleven
hours.* Once again, I checked my notes: Climb east side
of brook ten minutes NW of lean-to—eventually cross
brook to ridge to Seward summit. Compass reading
from brook: 218°.

I knew I was facing a long day of bushwhacking to

these three summits; that I'd be climbing, descending and climbing again, and retracing my steps on the way home. My estimated vertical ascent for the day was 4,500 feet. And while I knew I'd be exhausted at the end of the day, unless I lost my way or broke a leg I would reach my goal.

By six I found the brook that began the long climb up Seward. A surge ran through me as I turned into the woods. Behind me I heard a long, low rumble of thunder, but I carried a rain jacket and pants in my pack and thought I was prepared.

I followed the brook for a little over a mile before coming to a cairn, a small, neatly piled pyramid of stones, a sign from other climbers that this was where I should cross. I set down my pack, took a long drink of water and collected several small stones to add to the cairn. After picking my way from rock to rock across the brook, I climbed alongside it until I located a herd path that crossed the water again, then followed the northeast ridge. The path was steep and narrow and as I struggled up it, sharp pointed limbs cut and scratched my arms and legs.

I pushed on and, after three-and-a-half hours, reached the summit of Seward, its elevation of 4,361 feet clearly marked on the canister. I signed in, took my notes and read the log, finding, as I knew I would, Henri Vanier just ahead of me in June and on the summit the three preceding months. Nothing seemed to interfere with *his* pursuits.

I began a steep descent to the south, giving up all I'd

gained to reach the summit of Seward. I climbed down
and down until I thought I'd lost the herd path or missed
a sign that would direct me toward Donaldson. I reached
a rocky clearing from which I could see the steep cliffs I
was bypassing and Donaldson's round and thickly forest-
ed summit. It was the first open view of the mountains
I'd seen since leaving Ward Brook and it gave me an un-
familiar sense of freedom.

It began to rain, and thunder rolled in the mountains
north of me. I pulled on my rain jacket and baseball
cap, marked my line of travel and took a compass reading
of 222°, then referred to the azimuth I'd recorded on my
map: 226°. I was on course.

The climb down bottomed out and I began the as-
cent of Donaldson, re-entering the dense woods, sharp
branches noisily scraping my jacket as I crawled under
and over trees lying across my path. As I reached the
summit of Donaldson at 4,140 feet, the rain began to fall
heavily and the thunder crept closer. I hurriedly signed
in the log. The sky went white with lightning and thun-
der clapped behind me and I thought I must get off the
small summit quickly. I didn't need to check to see if I
was still following Henri Vanier. I knew I was.

I hurried down the ridge between Donaldson and
Emmons, encouraged that I'd reach my forty-sixth peak
within an hour, when lightning arched above me followed
by a deafening thunder crack. I ran off the ridge, fighting
through thick clusters of spruce and fir, unbuckling the
chest and belly bands on my pack as I ran. I struggled to
get farther from the crest, and pulled my arms free of my

pack straps. A sharp branch jabbed me in the left cheekbone, stopping me in place. I reached with my free hand to see how badly I was hurt. Blood ran freely down my dirty, wet fingers.

I stopped in a stand of spruces with no tall trees to attract lightning, set my pack on the ground, sat on it, then pulled my knees to my chest and held them in place to keep my body and feet off the ground. I tucked my head in my arms and watched blood drip from my cheek onto my shorts.

The next lightning strike dove brilliantly into the mountainside closer than the one before, no more than a quarter of a mile north of me. As the thunder's echo rolled through the mountains the noise of the rain resumed, hard against my hunched back. *If lightning kills me, how long will it take before they find me? What will Melanie say when she's told I've been killed one summit short of my goal?*

I didn't want someone else to tell her. I wanted to tell her myself. Tell her I was sorry. *I'm losing it. You can't tell her if you're dead. But maybe she'll understand.*

Then I heard her parting words: "I hope this gets it out of your system."

I waited.

Lightning lit the dark clouds with a white phosphorescence. The hair on the sides of my head lifted on end, a humming filled my ears.

All went black.

Silent.

Sometime later, I found myself lying in a rivulet of rain-
water that ran under and around me down the mountain.
I could feel the rain but couldn't hear it. I saw lightning
in the distance but couldn't hear the thunder.

My pack lay a few feet from me. I crawled toward
it. The silence was dizzying. An arm's length from my
pack I vomited in a strong, liquid stream. Lightning
flashed again without a sound.

I dragged my pack toward me. The shoulder straps
were still intact but the back of the pack was spread open
as if it had been ripped with a saw. My Gatorade and
two plastic water bottles were split from cap to bottom.
My rain pants, polar-fleece vest, first-aid kit, Swiss Army
knife, bottle of Deet, and tube of sunscreen were fused in
a wet mass of pile and plastic. All that was left were my
map and wool cap.

I was trembling and knew I must find a way to
warm myself. I replaced my rain-soaked baseball cap
with my wool cap and waited for my body temperature
to respond. I checked my fingertips to see if I'd been
burned. *I'm okay there*, and felt the cut beneath my eye.
It had swollen into a hard knot, but had stopped bleed-
ing. My trembling slowed, my head began to clear, and I
began to hear the rain falling on my jacket, then thunder
to the south.

*What now? What would Melanie want? What would
Vanier do? Finish? Turn back?* I tied together what was
left of my pack and stood, hoping for a sign, but the close
cluster of spruces shielded me from all but the steadily
falling rain and the lightning and thunder that drifted

through the mountains. Then I heard Melanie's advice: "It's not the destination, it's the journey that counts," and I answered her aloud, "But I'm so close. I've got to get it out of my system." Even as I said it, I wasn't sure it was the right choice.

I struggled back to the ridge on clumsy legs that felt like they belonged to someone else and followed the herd path toward Mt. Emmons, working hard to raise my body temperature, to get back in control. Within half an hour I reached an intermittent stream bed. I cupped my hands and drank from the rain water that ran freely over it before climbing alongside it toward the summit.

I'd scrambled no more than 200 yards over the slick rocks and small slides when my hands and boots lost their hold and I fell against a jagged rock, opening a gash to my shin bone. I rolled on my side, grabbed my leg with both hands and pulled my knee hard against my chest until the pain partially subsided. *God, I'm glad I'll never have to do this again.* I stood and washed the blood from my hands and my shin in the stream, and began to pull myself over the rocks once again.

The rain eased to a drizzle and from the top of the stream bed I could see a gray light through the trees above me and knew I was close to reaching my goal. Now that I was almost there, I wondered why it had seemed so important to me. I fought my way upward through thick woods, then followed the herd path as it made a sharp turn to the right and climbed at a 45° angle to the summit. I stopped in the small opening, surrounded by stunted spruces and balsam firs, and stared at the canister with EMMONS painted vertically on it in red letters, and decals of French and Canadian flags placed on either side. *Vanier's work?* I wondered. I dropped the remains of my pack and wearily raised my fists above my head. "I've finished! I've done it!" I said, but wondered if it was worth all that it took; if it was the big deal I'd made it out to be.

I slowly drew the log from the canister, sat on the wet ground, took my notes and signed in for the last time: "June 24, 1998. 12:50 PM. Bret Miller. Saratoga Springs NY. Finally! Number 46! Other than being struck by lightning on Donaldson, it's been a pretty uneventful climb." I began to write, 'Henri Vanier, can you match that?' but before I'd finished writing his name, I crossed it out.

Weak-limbed and light-headed, I took in the misty, gray view of a lake in the distance. *I'd better keep moving. The climb back over Donaldson and Seward will put me at the lean-to close to dark. Closer to Melanie.* I put the log away without looking for Vanier's entries, knowing they were there, and began the long hike home.

I arrived at the Ward Brook lean-to wet, cold, hungry. Katie and Michael's gear was gone, making the shelter look very empty. I wished they'd been there so I could tell them about my day, and make me feel less alone.

Hurriedly, I changed into dry clothes, lit a fire, wrapped my sleeping bag across my shoulders and brewed a cup of tea laced with honey. I massaged the cut on my shin. It was already a bluish-black and swollen to the size of a walnut and had begun to throb. The knot under my eye ached at my touch. I swallowed two Advil with my tea, and thought, *Cuts and bruises are a small price to pay. I could be below the ridge of Donaldson, dead where I might never be found. Dead without Melanie ever knowing all that had changed.* I thought about how and what I'd tell her, imagined holding her close to me, and I wondered if she'd push away or press against me the way she used to.

I cooked supper, cleaned up quickly and zipped myself into my sleeping bag, exhausted. The bag's closeness and warmth were a comfort, and a feeling of satisfaction mixed with relief came over me. *I've finished. It's over.* As I slipped into sleep I imagined Melanie pulling me to her, laughing with me.

At daybreak I began the hike to the trailhead, walking slowly. I let out a deep breath and smiled. I didn't have a schedule to keep, a goal to meet. I studied the trees, sugar maples, beeches, yellow birches, and hemlocks, and marveled at how beautiful they were. They breathed wetly as they woke with the morning sun, filtering the sunlight on the trail in soft, bright blotches.

I reached the trail register and checked out, and started to close the book when I noticed that mine was the last name written in it. Katie and Michael hadn't signed themselves in, or out.

31

Flood On Giant Mountain, June 29, 1963

By Pamela Lee Cranston

EVERYONE SCATTERED from the wedding like confetti as the windy thunderheads roiled up from the south like storm troopers or a pair of angry stepsisters, snubbed by someone who inconveniently forgot to invite them to the party. We watched as the black clouds glowered and seethed over Giant, then raced home as silver pellets bombarded our car—wet shrapnel bursting from the bowels of booming cannon.

Heavy downpour: four inches in two hours. A sudden backlog dammed up Giant's Washbowl, then burst its banks, thrusting a plow of boulders and torn trees over Roaring Brook Falls. It scythed the open field and felled the white pines along the highway as if a snake of brown sludge had slithered from its lair and swallowed huge chunks of macadam road whole, the way a snake gobbles up a gray mouse with one gulp.

We never know when the Brown River of big moments will come crashing upon us. Life wields the harrower's blade when we least expect it—forcing us to grow or die standing still.

I remember watching my father as he hoisted himself into his fishing waders, pulled on his rubber poncho and set out, armed just with a flashlight, through the black rain towards the torrent that surged past our orchard where the wild crabapples grow. He helped one couple climb out of their sinking car just as the Chevy next to them floated like a dinky toy slowly downstream. He found other campers stranded on high ground and led them home—like a band of drenched sheep. Rescue teams rushed from Keene Valley and forged human chains across the raging road. One man, salvaging a scrawny woman from her tossed car, slipped and nearly washed away with her. Arms thrashed, bodies lunged, but they were caught and saved.

Next day, the clear sky knelt down all sorry and blue, full of remorse, even as the forest's wreckage gushed all around us. Corpses of beech and hemlock lay strewn everywhere, like huge stems of shriven straws. Bones from an army of twisted oaks poked from the silt like frozen arms of dead soldiers reaching out from the muddy morgues of Flanders or Passiondale. The sweet stench of gashed trees, ripe as the carcass of a rotted fox, polluted the air worse than the pulp mills past Tupper Lake.

That day, I knew something terribly mortal, a deep wound, had happened here—as if Nature, in sullen despair, had savaged her own wrists.

Meanwhile, our small band of survivors huddled together, dried our sodden clothes by the stoked fire, and told our stories over and over. How the beer in the ice chest was found and the wire glasses surfaced, all unscathed. Dazed but grateful to be alive, we partied into the night, turning our fear into festival. And I wondered how long it would take for the earth to heal—(as we humans so rarely can do), and ached for the tender land that had raped itself.

Climbing Down Dix Mountain

Licking salt off my lip,
I clambered down
the top of Dix,
sucking thin air
musky from pitch
melting in the throbbing sun.
My canteen,
moist as cold stone,
clanked against my hip.

Down at timberline
where the scrub pine grows,
my boots bit
the soft duff of earth,
springy as eiderdown,
and busted up a den
of sleeping bees.

Yellow Jackets, sizzling
with daggers of terror,
pierced holes in a place
I never knew I carried.

All denial punctured,
I sank down by the trail

upon my own burden
and spilled a hot
bag of tears—

like some vagrant
carrying molten marbles
for sale.

—*Pamela Lee Cranston*

Canoeing into the Past

By Edward Ford

I REMEMBER THE TENACIOUS freshness of summer: the red morning sun reaching through the dazzling Maine woods, and the clouds of bug spray that I sprayed on my arms. My knees poked out of the holes in my jeans, and I sprayed them too, and then zapped my feet until the mosquitoes flew in harmless, hungry circles over my head. I remember the pine needles and the prickly pine conelets sticking to my toes and to the soles of my feet as I walked to the mooring by the old hemlock tree that arched over the black water of the cove. Depositing my gear in the nape of the tree's neck I leapt out onto the long granite rock that served as a dock for my old wooden canoe, a last remnant of the 19th century that had slipped away from my great-aunt and into my possession.

A spider rested on the seat. Gingerly, I offered him the tip of the paddle, then flipped him off onto the water's surface where he sprawled for a moment before scrambling back to shore. A few passes with the milk-carton bailer and the night's seepage was removed and the gear stowed in the prow: peanut butter and jelly sandwich for lunch, thermos of iced tea, raisins, fishing rod and lure, life preserver, sketchbook and pencils. After raising the old window-sash weight that served as an anchor, I took my seat in the stern, pressed the paddle against the rock, and pushed off.

Gliding out from under the hemlock branches, I entered a cloud of mist. Vapor curtains swept across the prow. I slid forward fearlessly, having previously mapped out every rock, stump, and lily-pad colony in the cove, and having become familiar with the canoe's habits: how it behaved in the waves, its whims in the wind, and its three-inch draw which allowed me to explore secret marsh passages that were inaccessible to other boats. Likewise, the oak paddle had long been worn to sit smoothly in my palm.

Drifting through the fog, I passed the submerged trunk of a tree that raised an index finger up out of the water. Along with a chain of stumps extending from the opposite shore, this underwater giant guarded the mouth of the cove from the depredations of passing motor boatists and made it seem as if it really was "my" cove. Off to starboard was a stand of pitch pines on Indian Point along with the shattered gray remains of the broken trees that had been struck by lightning. A woodpecker began slamming his head against one of the silver, barkless trunks and, spotting his red head through a hole in the mist, I set my paddle down soundlessly, dropped anchor, and took out my sketchbook.

The fog gave way in the maize-colored light as I reached the open lake. Once a river, then a pond, the lake was formed in 1792 when the town dam was built in order to create a log run. The surrounding forest has been logged periodically ever since; the last time being in the 1950s, shortly before I was born. The logs were floated down the length of the nine-mile lake to the dam where the sawmills were once stationed. What remains of the mill buildings have become home to swallows, mice, and to the occasional maple sapling sprouting up through the floorboards.

The logs were cut into planks and loaded onto flatbed cars at the local railroad spur which has long since disappeared, having been torn up and sold to a Massachusetts firm for use in an amusement park, which is now closed, too. The logs were also cut and fashioned right on the premises into desks, tables, chairs, and boards. In fact, the entire town had been literally "carved" out of the forest: the churches, the taverns, the general store with the second floor apartment and the big green IGA logo on the side, the firehouse containing the town's lone fire engine and, most of all, the long farm houses with the curled lattice work and the expansive verandas that are now gray and warped and crying out for rain. They even built the old dance hall where, on a Saturday night, the work week could be shaken off on a modern springed dance floor.

Hugging the left bank, I peered down into the water to glimpse the submerged wall of a shed. The headland that I was passing had once been home to a match factory, and it was still dominated by two piles of sawdust. Over time, the heaping mounds had spread out across the main body of the peninsula and had begun spilling down into the water; and it was on this slow moving tide of sawdust that the wall had ridden until it had finally been carried underwater along with countless boards, cans,

and contorted iron contraptions that were once used for
God knows what: pipes, gears, cranks, wheels, poles. . . .
On the far side of the sawdust piles the main body of the
peninsula was a flat downy plain that was only marked
by a dirt road that curved down towards town.

At the top of the headland a tangle of oaks had some-
how resisted the incursions of both loggers and the ad-
vancing sawdust desert. A cluster of birch saplings lined
the shore and stretched out over the water; some of the
more reckless had already plunged in. Spread out across
the birch branches like the tasseled hangings of an old-
fashioned bed lay a canopy of grape leaves and brown
hairy vines. Ducking under this curtain I entered a green
tunnel lit by dazzling streaks of sunlight. Great big
bunches of Concord grapes hung from the vines: some
green, some reddish purple and, reaching down, I in-
spected the few bunches that were ripening underwater.

Slipping out of the arbor and rounding the headland I
looked out across the lake to the crags of Picket's Hill.
Once there was a watchtower on top which commanded a
sweeping view of the mountains to the north, and off to
the west towards the nearby pond that was the site of
Lovell's famous fight. On the far shore there is a 1904
Daughters of the American Revolution stone marker that
bears the date May 25, 1725 and it lists the names of the
twelve colonials who came up from Massachusetts and
who died along with Chief Paugus and his Pequawket
warriors in the day-long skirmish. For you see, the silent
forests and redolent hills of today were once hotly dis-

puted property. And Ensign Wyman must surely have headed off in this direction as he lead the survivors on their long midnight march.

I was alone on the lake; and its still surface reflected white cotton cumuli as they lolled their way up over the peak. The canoe slid across the taught lake-skin. Plunk! The paddle struck the water like a drumstick and the sound reverberated against the hillside.

Tensing my back muscles I heaved a mighty stroke, lifted the paddle, then turned my shoulders around to watch the pair of whirlpools spin off in the wake. A sharp backstroke brought the canoe to a halt and created another pair of whirlpools right by my side. Lowering my hand into the swirling waters I imagined the horror of the plankton as they were sucked down into the vortex of my miniature maelstrom. The water was cold and clear, but thick with pond life. The swirls dissipated and the lake grew calm once more.

Until a mighty stroke launched me on my way.

I remember directing the canoe towards a particular gorse bush that concealed a slender break in the shoreline. A tangle of sheep laurel and golden rod twigs extended over the prow; and, drawing them back gently, I entered into what seemed a primordial swamp.

Weathered gray stumps sat regally on mounds, dipping their toes in the water, and letting their Dr. Seuss hair sprout out wildly. Some peeped their heads up out of the water to contemplate their young friend. Others donned huckleberry bushes and modestly concealed their torsos beneath the water, while still others posed beneath the surface and smirked up at me through my reflection. It looked as if they were all originally cut to about the same height, but, as with the jagged crowns of candles, time had burned each of them differently so they continued to assert their individuality, long after having lost their vitality.

The water covered the blade of the paddle, and the bottom was a cushion of leaves and muck that was just as deep again. Walking sticks and water boatmen scampered across the dusty surface. Here it was best to travel like a Mississippi raftsman: standing strong and alert in the stern.

A single path threaded its way through the swamp, a path which I had created myself by pushing aside those troublesome logs which would raise one end up to the surface while nestling the other end down in the muck. It was closed off from the main lake by a curving bank that was lined with reeds, Indian wort, and towering pines whose tops were but tufts against a Van Ruisdale sky. Spiders sailed through the air holding onto their filaments; and a kingfisher alighted silently on a branch. But it was only after discovering a water rat dozing on a moss covered log that I put down the paddle and took up my sketchbook.

Leaving the swamp behind, I steered over to a pair of coves that had once served as docking bays for the old match factory. Up ahead, off the starboard bow, was a pine island with its brown needle carpet extending down to the shore. A string of ramshackle cottages stretched out along the road that ran down the spine of the island and over the stone bridge to the edge of town where an old printed sign read *Pinegrove Cottages—Vacancy*. Built log cabin style back in the 1950s the houses were now battered and empty: chimneys dripping off the roofs, screen doors splayed out in the yards.

Most people did not know that the cottages were situated on an island, but the narrow channel of water separating it from the main body of the peninsula gave it island status. The channel's straight banks were covered with mosses and ferns that unfurled their viols out over the water. The channel grew brighter as you progressed through it; as the omnipresent pines gave way to birch and maple saplings; and as the strip of sand along the bank submerged itself in a marsh of cat tails, purple iris, black alder, and assorted reeds. For a few moments the canoe crashed its way through the grasses until, bursting out of the channel, it emerged at the top of a tear-drop shaped pond.

A dirt road along the shore connected the town of Denmark with the sawdust piles; and there was a sprawling farm house that constituted the edge of town. In its backyard there was a great millstone in a bright tulip garden; and a parched dock that stretched its lip down towards the water. All across the surface of the pond the reflections of the dock, the farm house, and the pines were mottled by lily-pad clusters blooming in yellow, white, and orange. Beneath the lily pads were schools of minnows, lurking; while up above a hawk was circling in the sky.

Algae and skunk-weed were plentiful, and I could sense the presence of frogs. Painted turtles were sunning themselves on the stones and stumps lining the shore, craning their orange striped necks up to observe me with their reptilian eyes. The rocks on which they sat were lined down the middle with yellow stripes of pollen, separating their sun-bleached tops from their water-stained torsos.

By the stone bridge stood a brown, ginger-bread-house style restaurant building. After swimming lessons, when I was younger, I used to sit on a stool at the bar—it was always empty, the air dusty, and the stave chairs set up on the tables—and drink vanilla milk shakes and smile beneath my milk-shake mustache while my mother sipped iced tea.

I took out my Thermos and sipped some iced tea, then took out my sketchbook and began drawing.

Writing in 1852 Thoreau remarked that in Maine "immigration is a tide which may ebb when it has swept away the pines" and today's forests support his observation. While out walking one day I climbed over a moss-covered wall into an old wood lot where the underbrush had been cut to make room for snowmobile trails. At first I was saddened to see the woods treated in such a manner, but then, looking back at the stone wall, I remembered that much of the region had once been cleared for farming.

CANOEING INTO THE PAST

Other times, other ways, and the land which once met a
need for food was now satiating a need for recreation. In
fact, not fifty years ago there were actually fewer trees in
the area than there were at present; for back then the
entire region was an agricultural powerhouse the full
extent of whose capacities can be judged by the sheer size
of the hilltop farm houses, protected by stolid elms and
sporting curving cornices and even modest towers, over-
looking sloping yellow fields and round duck ponds.

It is not just the size of the farms that is impressive,
but also their silence, which matches that of the distant
blue hills. Only a few of the farms are still cultivated,
their fields dotted with hay bales that resemble giant
plastic marshmallows. Atop the barn roofs the old, golden
weather vanes are still to be seen evoking bright economic
forecasts of days gone by: painted copper horses, arrows,
roosters, full-rigged ships, banners, owls, locomotives,
foxes, heraldic angels, horse-drawn fire engines, or a heart
and thistles. All these shapes and the variety of gilded
details remind us just how central nature was to daily
life. A dry northeast wind meant a good day for haying;
and regularly, throughout the course of the day, farm
hands would glance up from their work to the cardinals at
the base of the vane to see the N-E-W-S.

Arriving at the stone bridge I leapt out of the canoe
and dragged it up on shore where the sand had dried in
the shape of rippling wavelets. I sat down on a log behind
the crumbling restaurant, took out my lunch and began
eating.

A pair of dragonflies hovered overhead, then flew out

over the pond.

After a time my mother came walking down the road. She had been to town and carried a brown paper bag out of the top of which protruded the brown and yellow hairs of several ears of corn. She sat down on the log, and I offered her iced tea.

We did not talk as we ate. But we often spoke at other times when I would listen attentively to my mother's stories about the old family farm in Ohio and about how the family fortune had gone the way of my Great Uncle John: He had been a famous gambler on the Mississippi steamboats. About how the family had originally come from Massachusetts where it had been vaguely, quite vaguely, rather extremely vaguely related to the Lincolns; but had then moved west along with General Israel Putnam and his wagon train to the Ohio River Valley in the years that followed the American Revolution. I remember my mother's telling me about her grandfather's Grandfather Ben riding west at the age of eight; and how he had told the story to his grandson who had told it to my mother who then told it to me.

And as it was in Ohio, so it was here in Maine. With their new-found freedom the colonists began the push westward into the great North American forest; and enough of them had filtered up the dusty back roads of Maine to incorporate a town here in 1807.

Lunch over, I picked up the trash and climbed back into the canoe. I sat in the stern seat, Mother sat up front, the groceries sat in the middle. We slid under the stone bridge, crouching down so as to avoid the giant spiders that went dashing across the underside of the brigde, and emerged at the end of the lake where the water roared over the dam. Off to starboard was the pine island, off to port was the green slope of Picket's Hill; ahead were the rounded, blue mountains in the distance, and the ardent summer sky opened out over our heads. And all the while, surging beneath us and stretching out before us like a sparkling blue sheet, lay the main body of the lake.

Plunk! A mighty paddle stroke launched us on our way.

The canoe trip 'round the headland was always safe and simple and it usually had a clear purpose: for example one could easily conclude that the twin goals of the trip were to pick up my mother after shopping and to do some sketching along the way. But, as I can see now, and as I guess I knew vaguely back then, the practical aims of the trip were, in the end, rather unimportant. For the importance of such trips is not to be measured by a certain number of miles or described by the inarticulate series of sketches that I collected along the way. Rather, there is something else, something less practical, less tangible, something beyond emotion and intellect; something which, even though I could not define it (perhaps "experience" is a good approximation), nevertheless I knew that it was both "real" and "important" because I could feel it burning inside me, deep down inside of me, urging me on to something bigger, something farther, something grander, something that would end up sending me ranging out across the continent and draw me back to Maine again.

This inner sense of restlessness to which I am referring is probably attributable to the fact that my family moved a lot when I was a child. But through all the changes, my parents always kept the same summer house that had been built in the hopeful year of my birth and which still stands: a pine cabin with blue spruce stain and white trim; on a wooded hilltop in the fresh Maine air. In time I came to regard it as my true home: as a place of stability that was unlike the fleeting houses of our suburban hibernation.

It was from the granite rock under the old hemlock tree that I first ventured off on my own; just around the headland at first (that was a trip that I took quite often and which I still like to recall now that I am older); but then later up lake and beyond. And so, looking back on it, it seems as if all of my later adventures began there....

Maine Morning

In me, the stillness of the shore
the fullness of the lake
the light swinging over the water
above the tremor of wave
amid silence and space
the wholeness of the sky.

I shall shout against its void,
up, into its purity
pushing my voice and longing into its depth.
For sweet is the sound of the wave
the pulse of the heart's rising song
my oneness with the wind.

—David Napolin

'glorious mournful'

still pond: a dragonfly hums by.

a half-rotted log crumbles
me into the water.

a crow calls: caw-echoes bounce back;
one becomes a flock.

a thin sheet of bark floats outside
down on the water, gray frog
perched on top.

she adjusts herself and is still;
i follow suit.

—*Christopher Boone*

Lost on the Nantahala

By Virginia Rudasill Mortenson

CAROLINE STARES at Nantahala Falls, and quivers at the roar of the water.

Young men with lithe bodies wiggle kayaks against the riffles of the current. Out of one eddy, leaning, paddling over a wave to reach another. They line up at the bottom of the falls to whirl into the cascade.

Sometimes, they ride the maelstrom sideways like bucking a bronco in a rodeo. Or, they shoot straight up in the air, twist and flip upside down in the river. Then, they get in line to do it all over again.

Caroline tries to ignore Ernest's feet in rubber socks, bright red, resting on the boulder beside her. Above the tight blue legs of the wet suit, his words drop like stones on her head.

"You think I'm too old for this. Don't you? Be honest. Say it."

Without bothering to look up, she knows his lip juts out. *He's like a child*, she thinks. For almost thirty years, she's coped with his whims. And, his one-sided bickering. His roar churns up its own froth in her mind.

"Old? You're only fifty," she says. *Grow up*, she wants to shout over the noise. "Don't tell me you're going to chicken out after coming all this way? And all the lessons. . . ?"

Except for the pull of the van's engine, they drive in silence. Kudzu vines drape the mountain side on the left. Below them on the right, the Nantahala River races to the falls and on to Lake Fontana.

Ahead of them an old school bus, painted blue, turns into the entrance of the put-in park. Some kids stick their paddles out the back windows. They wave and yell at no one. The glow of their bright orange life jackets penetrates the mud crusted over the windows. Six-person rafts jiggle on top of the bus.

"I know you think this is stupid." Ernest jerks on the emergency brake. While he unties the ropes holding the purple kayak on top of the van, she watches children spill from the bus.

A man with a stomach almost as big as Ernest's, with legs just as skinny, blows a whistle. The children, all boys, circle him.

Ernest groans. The kayak wobbles over his head. As he twists his body and sets the kayak on the grass, a boy twists his body away from the group to watch Ernest. Downs Syndrome.

Caroline looks out the other window. Beside them a bumper sticker stuck on an Escort's paint says, GRACE HAPPENS!

"You don't have to watch me go," Ernest says over his shoulder. He kneels over the kayak.

Caroline eases herself from the passenger seat over the road maps to Ernest's faded spot behind the steering wheel.

"Oh, here's my watch." Ernest stands. "11:00

now." He drops the watch through the open window onto her lap.

"Should be at the falls by one. You can take my picture coming over," he shouts as he shimmies his head into the red helmet. He turns away from her and waves.

She clicks the key in the ignition and reads a sign through the windshield: *Life Jackets Required.* "You have your life jacket?" she calls to him.

He raises his arms and flings them outward, the way she's seen him do a thousand times. "Oh, my God. No! Good thing you remembered."

By the time she drives over the bridge to park at the Nantahala Outdoor Center, it's raining. Under her black umbrella she buys a cup of coffee through the outdoor window of Slow Joe's Cafe and walks to a picnic table beside the river.

Though Caroline feels the wetness of the bench through her shorts, she doesn't move. She stares over the riffles and through the slalom poles to the store, the back of which borders the other side of the river. *When I finish this coffee, I'll shop,* she thinks. *I'll buy some postcards— the ones I want—maybe, a shirt. Ernest can't stop me.*

Where is he at this minute? she wonders. *Has he tipped over?* She decides that if it's still raining at 1:00, she won't take the video camera with her to the falls.

Caroline decides not to buy postcards. Not one picture looks like the real thing, the real Nantahala, to her. Besides, her friends in Iowa wouldn't be impressed. So silly to waste the money. Ernest wouldn't believe her thriftiness.

By 12:00 she is waiting under her umbrella at Nanta-
hala Falls. Five young kayakers *surf the holes*, she says to
herself, having picked up on the lingo bantered around
her. Everyone seems young, babies almost with bodies
bending this way and that above bare feet. Water-
darkened hair drips over tanned faces. Some shiver—boys
with arms crossed in front of naked concave chests—girls
peering from under hoods of beach towels. "Cold, Man."

With her free hand Caroline pulls the thick sweater
from Mexico around her ample chest. She's glad Ernest
wore his wet suit. She wonders if he already ate the tuna
sandwich he packed in the pink neon bag this morning in
their trailer, which is parked at the camp site. *At least he
does for himself these days*, she thinks.

Settling herself into a rock indented to a perfect fit,
she watches the parade of kayakers sliding with the water
over the falls. More rafts now than earlier bump against
rocks to careen over the rollers. Each group has a
screamer aboard, some have more than one, louder than
the roar of the waves.

The kayaker's line at the bottom of the falls is longer
and before the next raft appears around the bend, another
kayak springs into action like a wind-up toy. She realizes
that each is trying to remain in a vertical position longer
than the other—*squirting*. She tries to imagine Ernest
squirting.

A two-person ducky that looks like an inflatable
plaything for a swimming pool starts over the falls. As its
nose sinks into the froth, its back hikes up, pitching the
man behind into the air. He crashes into the water and

disappears from sight.

Caroline gasps, but he quickly surfaces. Then, he grins at the audience on the boulders like he's a porpoise at Sea World. Everyone laughs, except Caroline. Everyone, except Caroline, seems to know him. "Goofy does it every time!" a young woman shouts.

By 12:45 the raft with the same children Caroline watched at the put-in park rumbles and bumps over the falls. All the children squeal except the boy with Downs Syndrome. He stares with no change of expression even when an arc of river slaps his face.

Caroline squirms, as if the boy's look is an omen, and she thinks about calling out to the guide—*Have you seen an old man in a red helmet and a blue wet suit, carrying a pink neon bag in a purple kayak?* Her heart flutters. She says nothing. Rain drops thump the black umbrella.

Between 1:00 and 1:38, four red helmets shoot around the bend toward the falls. None attached to Ernest. With each red blob, Caroline's eyes rise up and her chest lifts—all her parts, in fact, seem to move upward, by themselves. When each kayak shows itself, blue or yellow or red, everything closes up again, even her teeth tighten together.

At 1:53, a red helmet above a purple kayak swirls into view. She wants to shout at all the onlookers. *There's my husband. There's Ernest.*

From above the falls Ernest's face looks like concrete. Caroline bites her lower lip. She stands. Ernest shoots through the conflagration upright—before he flips. The red helmet disappears under the purple slab, drifting.

Up! Up! she wants to shout. He wiggles halfway up, a flash of red, then falls back under the water.

"That guy's turned over," a kid monotones.

Help him! Someone help him.

But then she sees him surface—he's loose—free of the boat, and he is swimming to the shore opposite her high perch. She thinks she hears his voice, weak in the distance: "Catch that boat."

Caroline makes no sound, at least none that the punks around her can hear. *He's safe*, she thinks, stretching, acting bored, then gingerly stepping over rocks back to the parking lot.

As Caroline crosses the bridge, she looks down the river's edge to see if she sees Ernest or the kayak. No where. Nothing. *No—he wouldn't jump back into the river to save the boat—that stupid purple boat?*

Beneath her on both sides of the bridge the slalom poles dangle, red and green, for racing practice, Ernest explained earlier, when they were crossing the bridge in the van. It had been her first view of Wesser Falls, just beyond the poles. "Now, *those* falls no one goes over," he had said. "Should have a warning sign. I didn't even know about them last year until halfway through the week, one lesson left to go. I played around by those poles one week day when no one was there. Could just as easy have slipped right on over, never to be heard from again."

Caroline picks up her step. In the parking lot behind the van, his body is stooped, his head under the bumper, Ernest in his dripping blue wet suit, is muttering to himself.

"What's wrong?" she asks.

"What's wrong?" he shouts. "My kayak is lost! I'll never see it again! Give me the keys! I was trying to get at the spare. I didn't know where you were . . . get in. We got to find it."

Over the gravel next to the railroad track the van rumbles. Ernest growls, acting like he did when he was in his twenties, she thinks. When they first got married, he was hot-tempered with boundless energy, almost a wild man sometimes.

She clears her throat. "Maybe, someone found it. . . ."

"Hell, no, no one got it. I saw it go over Wesser Falls with my own eyes. Probably smashed to bits or stuck forever in those rocks."

The words explode out of his mouth; his eyes bulge; his cheeks wobble all-red like a Richard Nixon imitator and his hair sticks up in wet spikes all over his head. Caroline feels like laughing—really laughing. She turns her head away from him toward a mountain covered with kudzu and tucks her lower lip under her top lip. Her eyes burn.

In and out of the van to check the river's edge, up and down below Wesser Falls. They speed around mountain curves and pull up at the clearing by the lake. Ernest jumps out, running. He tells the story to a Nantahala kayak instructor in front of her beginning kayakers. "Do you think it would have come into the lake? Do you know where the river meets the lake? I'm worried my kayak may have gotten smashed. Or lost. . . ."

Caroline leans against the van and begins to laugh, no longer able to keep her own riffles under control. She feels Ernest behind her.

"Caroline? What're you laughing about?" Ernest's words add more coal to her laughter. She doubles up—screeching, howling. Tears flow down her face. She can't stop herself long enough to breathe. Even the thought of Ernest flying into a rage doesn't stop her.

And, then, to her utter amazement, she hears above her own noise, Ernest laughing too. "God, it's so embarrassing!" he howls.

Later, back in the van, Caroline says, "I don't know why it's so funny, Ernest. Maybe, I'm just relieved it's only that purple boat and not you."

At 4:20, after over two hours of searching, down a path guarded by wild dogs, through weeds—*probably poison ivy*, she thinks, Ernest calls to her:

"Honey, I found her! She's caught in a fallen tree."

Once the kayak is retrieved, and strapped up on top of the van, Ernest winks over at Caroline. "I never lost anything before. Makes me think about what I'd do if I lost you."

He acts like such a child, she thinks, patting his hand.

Blue Heron

In the still coves of the Colorado, soft as twilight,
    a Blue Heron
tiptoes around sharp, green sticks, picking and choosing
    from the muddy tangles
fat frogs, tender grubs, and contentment.
The gentle currents unfasten my body, liberating
me from the usual pain, pulling me into azure arms,
shouldering my sorrows, carrying them downstream.
    I slip
above all of this aching flesh, drifting
on the moment's mercies,—
                    while the heron, lifting
                        and bowing, searches
                                through the slashing reeds.

Coyote

"I don't know what an angel looks like," he told me with
    his eyes shooting sparks
from the blue rivers on which they were floating. We sat
    cross-legged
on his blanket, making conversation, as I pawed-over
his arrowheads, fetishes, and animal skins.

The coyote ran out from the sage, surprising
my feet onto the brake. He stopped in the middle
of the road, opening me with knife

of its eyes for an eternal moment
on the Aha Macave reservation.

He fashioned arrowheads with a deer-bone chisel
and a bow, reviving the old ways. Shapeshifting
war stones into necklaces, undoing
the natural order of things—
I had only seen . . .

Coyotes at those in between times; in between dawn and
    morning,
in between dusk and moonlight, something must be
    driving him
into daylight, driving him out of the safety
of shadows—There he stood in the road, rippling
inside waves of heat, like a mirage.

I suppose some would call this man "crazy," with that
    earmarked hat
and those leathered hands, digging through scorched earth
for perfect stones. His wisdom was wily, not easily
    understood,
but I could hear it howling after me, as I left him, carrying
    away full pockets, my eye
jutting over my shoulder at him, unwavering in the sun.

The coyote released me from his scrutiny, glancing off
into the desert, he flicked his tail, and trotted away
towards shadows, to lie in wait
for darkness and light to set another rendezvous
in the middle of the road.

Swimming with the Moon
(*for Mary*)

The moon swims here almost every night, small stars
    flutter
around her, like white moths. Ebony currents tug
at her silvery ribbons, wrapping them around their wakes,
their silky threads slip over sandbars and black stones.

From the shoals, small villages of animals, come crawling
    and floating.
I quiver at the edges, as wind flaps the yellow wing of my
    hair.
My words ripple across the stillness—"This would be
    enough.
The river, the night's dark drowse." Soft fingers of silence

uncoil my competition, emptying all my enmity into the
    eddies, and muscles
too rigored to climb anymore ladders, begin to drape
from shoulders, like satin sleeves.
Maybe I am giving up,

or maybe I am just at the end of it.
Who defines those important things like Success. Anyway,
I have synonyms of my own. What about Colorado,
Cassiopeia, or Moonlight, or even better, Peace?

I think I could be happy being a river, pouring myself
    into nothing,
or the sand, shifting comfortably under the nuzzling of
    the wind,
or maybe the moon suspended over night's glossy window,
having the one thing I have always wanted—a perfect
    view.

The Rainbow Benediction

poem & essay By Thomas J. King

Was this not real? Then may its swindle reign,
its sham etch deep before the dark descends.
This river canyon hosts our band of friends
and here we taste a joy and barter pain

till moments laughing, rapt, intense, serene,
work memory's stops to thoughts which presage death—
a dram the heart drinks, summoning every breath
and glance and word which future mind may glean

of these enrichments, rare and unforeseen,
disarming time, though destined not to last,
comprised of miracles among us passed
by which we learn what life was meant to mean

beneath this dazzling arch that, after rain,
emblazons hues all common sense defy
hinting that God with temptress Earth hath lain
and must unscroll his bliss against the sky.

THE RIVER CANYON celebrated by this poem is so interwoven with the prime years of my life that I feel towards it like a member of my family. Real nature lovers don packs and hiking shoes and penetrate the myriad national parks and wildernesses of the American west. As an outdoorsman I'm entirely pseudo, a sedentary cerebral suburbanite. But once every summer black, thick, simian hair bushes out over my chest; it's time for the annual trek up the one and only canyon! And it's no easy feat to arrive below the hallowed falls where tradition marks the spot. What trails there are along the banks are sporadic and clogged with tree limbs. Sometimes sheer cliffs lift from the water's edge. It becomes necessary to cross and re-cross the water, negotiating the powerful current and slippery rocks underfoot while encumbered by massive backpacks. For these difficulties there is a great reward: isolation. The hike is too daunting for most other swarming suburbanites. This gorgeous canyon, replete with rushing water, pools wide and deep enough to satisfy any swimmer, achingly beauteous vistas and waterfalls, is situated only an hour or two by car from one of the nation's intense population hubs, and yet my wife and I have on occasion spent entire days within its breathstopping splendors without the encumbrance of a single article of clothing.

The remembrances collected within these idyllic parameters are too dramatic, too rich, to slip even from my sieve-like memory. There was that day, three of our kids still school children, we first allowed them into the sacred mystery. Their excitement was great, and I remember my surprise at how nimbly they managed the ascent. One of my reminiscences of that day was stumbling onto magnificent bevies of butterflies, it being that time of year one found them congregating for ephemeral purposes. Such massive air-mountings of vertiginous beauty that it hurt the heart. Then there was that first moment at the edge of the stream when I threw out a dare to the children—"Last one in the water is a monkey's uncle!" The next instant saw all three racing towards the shallow but icy arm of the American River. But our respective daughters threw on the brakes, while Kevin, my son, the youngest and therefore most gullible, plunged all the way in. It was so chilling, he screamed.

There was the sinister legend, hard come by, of the whirlpool. My wife's son Dan took a friend up on their own private expedition. In the swim, his friend, Steve Bridges, was caught in the tow of a whirlpool that wasn't just playful. Again and again he was sucked under, and as he periodically surfaced, Dan tried to catch him by the hand. Only when Steve's powers of holding his breath under water were nearly exhausted did he finally succeed. There had been times during that trial when Dan was sure Steve was a goner. He marveled, later, how his level-headed friend refused to panic.

There was the great race. The party was formed of Dan, Tom, Dar, and their friend John. We had our hearts set on grilling ourselves a hot meal that day, but arrived at The Traditional Spot only to realize we had left the matches in the car. Both Dan and John volunteered to go back down for the matches, and we got to considering who could make the roundtrip more swiftly. Dan, a natural athlete and fitness buff, was in the very prime of his twenties, and John was as goatfooted as some centaur, but a whole generation older. It seemed that Dan was the

logical choice--but males will be males. So they would
both go, making it a race! When they arrived back with
the matches, they had reduced the time required for the
distance to a fraction we wouldn't have believed if we
hadn't been there as witnesses. John won by a nose.

There was the tale of Laurel Nelson and the wedding
ring. She was secretly considering termination of her
fifteen-year marriage to her husband Richard, when by a
Freudian blunder she dropped her ring into the depths
of the river's swirling waters. The next day Richard
returned with a friend, clambered up the canyon, dove
down, and actually recovered the ring. As for the mar-
riage, it would prove soon enough to be beyond recovering.

The Favorite Spot (which would shift somewhat with
the years, as determined by changes wrought by spring
torrents) was situated by a distance of a good city block
(note suburbanite terminology) from The Great Water-
fall. Whenever a newcomer was allowed into the hallowed
domains, he or she would be subjected to The Initiation.
This consisted in swimming the bone-numbing channel
against the resistance of a challenging current until the
falls were attained. The secret and holy rites which
would then be experienced cannot be revealed. I shall
only say that they were as awesome as any tribal ritual
and would usually leave the initiates shiveringly purple,
dazed—and merrily screaming!

Getting up and getting back down constituted a
whole separate wing of the legends. Sprained ankles,
broken ribs, a smashed coccyx entailed fabulous adver-
sities to be overcome in negotiation of the descent. And

then there was one unforgettable nocturnal folly. . . . Temperance came to Tomandar only late in life, and there was a well-established custom of packing enough bottles of champagne to launch a whole fleet of ships— just in case any ships should somehow appear in the canyon, and need launching. On one very romantic occasion when the Kings, up alone, had cavorted through the whole sun-wondrous day, they lost their sense of time and realized too late that darkness was falling. By the time they'd packed up and started down, night had fallen like a smothering blanket—a moonless night. Remember—no trails. Imagine the two of us, smashed out of our silly gourds on bubbly, feeling our way with the soles of our sneakers over the slippery rocks in the rushing stream— actually crawling in the shallows!—making that tortuous trek, long hours at our snail pace, down through total ob- liviating blackness!

But most of our best experiences did not leave tall tales to recount. The cryptic core of the formula was to take only the most cherished in our lives for a day in the canyon, and the best expeditions consisted of lolling and languishing, enjoying good talk with loved ones in the embrace of all that wondrous beauty. Cultivating good conversation being an art to which I was devoted, I in- vented a special game called "Triptichs," which was not nearly so keen on competitiveness as it was on getting the company beyond small talk into a comfortable sharing of where they lived. It was a game eliciting high returns of camaraderie. "Triptichs" afforded infinite variations. E.g., "Describe three different scenarios of what might be your perfect day," which were then to be guessed at in the endeavor to determine the player's personal favorite. One involved dreaming up three versions of the best future lifestyle. I thought my daughter Liesl took the all-time prize. She came up with a society in which it would be the expected thing that when people gathered socially, instead of shaking hands or hugging, they would automatically give one another long, delightful backrubs!

We were so used to having the canyon all to ourselves that we felt indignant if we came across anybody else. A small party of us "owners" were in our revels one day when we suddenly saw two young men making their way down the stream. We had brought a huge batch of cherries with us that day, and on impulse we commenced pelting the intruders—strangers we had never seen before—with our bings. They responded by catching them and popping them into their mouths!

One of the largest parties we ever took up with us arrived for the ascent in a van. We were fanned out injun-file, quietly traversing one of the portions of the safari with land underfoot, when I, in the lead, rounded a bend to encounter a most remarkable piece of scenery. It wasn't just that a woman with a gorgeous body, totally naked, suddenly struck my astonished gaze. It was the positioning of it all She was lying atop a flat boulder situated smack up against the path, so that she abruptly appeared at eye level and approximately an arm's length away. She had a blanket covering her head—but only her head. (It seemed that her modesty was ostrich-like.) Furthermore, she lay with her legs asprawl, so that one's *coup d'oeil*, delivered like a shotgun blast impacting at point blank range, was of a gaping orifice only somewhat provocatively adumbrated by a pubic bush. So there we paraded past, some dozen pilgrims, each one in turn coming to take the blast head-on. The silence of the moment was eerie.

A delicious follow-up is rounding out this mere moment into a choice anecdote. Our dear friend John had come over from San Francisco once again for the excursion, and we had arranged a blind date for him. The "fix," as is the case of these things more often than not, turned out to be a total flop. It told the whole story that on descending the canyon at the end of the day, the lady we had "fixed" him with was all the way at the front of the column, and John was back with me, bringing up the rear. When we came to the Station of the Flat Boulder, lo! the attractive young satyress supplementing the pleasure of our ascent was still there, enjoying the canyon in its crepuscular light, still wrapped in her solitude, but this time also in her blanket. Our hopes were confirmed that the anatomical *tour de force* nature had devised was crowned by a head mounted on a neck. "Hi!" we said. "Hi!" she replied. Followed by more hi's, approximately a dozen. We were passing on when I had an idea. It was an idea prompted by guilt after the abortive attempt to "fix up" my friend John. I took the remaining bottle of wine from my knapsack, put it in John's hands, and motioned towards the path down which we had just come. It was an exercise in perfect non-verbal communication, leaving John in a pool of reflection.

After a moment I looked over my shoulder, and discovered that John somehow had gotten separated from the group. When the party was assembled back at the van, I reported that we seemed to have lost John. After about an hour, John showed up. It was noticed with curiosity how his former gloominess had been ditched for a face full of silly smiles. He had returned not only with a memory of a very special bonus hour, but with a date, which was kept in the canyon on a later day.

The canyon was magical. Over the course of thirty years of frequenting it, I never experienced a day every hour of which did not fill me with the deepest gratitude for being alive and healthy, with all my senses gratified. And it was difficult to say of those days of such unbelievable bounty, which registered most, the sense of mind-boggling natural beauty or the sense of camaraderie in its midsts.

You must excuse me now. For as I strike these very keys, it is June 1st once again. Summer! "Beth—don't forget to put the t.p. in one of the backpacks. . . ."

Footsteps

When I first camped, I feared myself;
I thought my very presence could disturb
the wilderness, would harm the earth,
and so I stepped as lightly as I could
while berrying and always cringed
to see my footsteps on the broken stalks,
until I saw how bear smash swaths
to gorge themselves on first ripe blackberries
or how the raccoon mother fells
the whole raspberry plant to feed her young;
she bites the base, fells half the patch.
I forage now without remorse.
I worried about making too much noise,
before observing animals
far noisier than I—the crashing moose.
The mouse moves loudly in the midnight field;
I hear the slither of the snake.

Paths

When I was young, I made my paths,
and often I was sure, or else I guessed
as best I could and pressed ahead,
not striving for the straightest, fastest way:
I sought the best, most beautiful,
and thus I followed twisting forage trails
of moose and deer, or tried to track
the mostly vanished paths of other men,
detours around hollows . . . I blazed
by cutting deep, hacking limbs, painting bright,
and even as I made my marks
across a desert island wilderness,
I saw my paths as metaphor
for all my art and thought, and now,
the forest and the bog reclaim my toil.
I keep no trails; I blunder on
through thickets green beyond conclusion.

Backpacker

I slouch comfortably on a polished stone and
cast my gaze across the crystal waters
of the spring-swollen river
like an arcing line of six-pound test.
Wind-brushed snowdrifts,
a flash of forest green against
a cobalt sky frame the scene of
Nature's virgin splendor,
as flies devour
a recently thawed carcass,
bringing to mind twenty-thousand campers
on the other side of the hill.

— *Gordon Frank Rich*

A Bear Incident

By Uncle River

THE BLUE RIVER runs down the Arizona-New
Mexico state line through the largest of the South-
west's forested island ranges, which rise 10,000 to 12,000
feet out of the surrounding desert. Just a few feet wide
and a few inches deep that evening of the bear, in June,
the river offered more flowing water than any other in an
area 50 miles across, where I had lived 20 years as a her-
mit/writer in the Mountain Southwest, at about 6,000
feet, 13 miles from the pavement in Blue River Canyon.

The area is an anomaly, being one of the few places
on earth that had a substantially higher population 1,000
years ago than it does now. Today it is sufficiently wild
that the endangered lobo wolf has been reintroduced (a
subject of considerable local controversy). All sorts of
wildlife are common here, from beavers to crawdads in
the river to wild turkey and mountain lion in the forests.

Living here very simply, as Nature has allowed and
an almost total lack of money has required, I have had
the good fortune to be able to reflect on daily events as
elements in life's pattern. Such perspective, whatever it
may offer to human culture, long has seemed to me an all-
too-rare opportunity in our busy, noisy, distracted time.
Of course Nature does include some dramas and, in them,
I sometimes have found points of focus around which to
view patterns of life's history, both personal and collective,

by which to learn.

About 50 people live in the Blue River Canyon on small pieces of private property scattered along 30 miles of gravel road surrounded by thousands of square miles of National Forest: Ponderosa pine and oak on the slopes. Juniper and pinion. Cottonwood, walnut and willow brush by water. Aspen, fir and spruce up high. All tinder dry in the driest time of the second drought year in a row, following a decade mostly on the warm and droughty side.

The land I have had the privilege to caretake is the middle 20 of 60 acres of private property, divided into four pieces. Only one of the other three pieces of this stretch of private land is inhabited full time.

My neighbors, both full time and occasional, have real houses. My home is more primitive: An 8x12 free-standing room built of construction scrap, with a wood stove, where I write, read, and sleep, and a 7x12 trailer where I use the propane stove to cook. There is an old barn too, built of hand-hewn logs, where I store things—a lifetime's accumulation of paper mostly, and where I have a refrigerator. The trailer is about 10 feet northeast of the room, the barn about as far beyond the trailer. My 1963 Ford pickup, operable but not registered for lack of money at the time, was parked by the east end of the trailer and about 20 feet from the room.

My room has a glass pane door on the east and a big fixed window made of half a sliding glass door facing south toward a field and the driveway. The latch of the trailer door is gone, so I prop a 4x4 against it to keep it shut, which has sufficed for wind and raccoons. I have electri-

80

city, for light, computer for my writing, the refrigerator, and the little pump in the surface well that enables me to water a garden. I don't have a phone. I can hear the road across the river, but vegetation hides it from view in summer. Hours commonly pass without my hearing any-one on the road. None of my neighbors' houses or lights can be seen from here.

Often I go a week or more without seeing or speaking to anyone. But one Friday I happened to walk out the few hundred yards to my mailbox (delivery and pick-up three times a week) at mail time and said hello to Louis Smith, the mail route driver. He told me there was "a rogue bear" in the canyon that likely had torn up a calf one place and a dog another, farther on down. Drought, causing the acorn crop to fail and making all food scarce, always brings bear problems.

Next day I rode to Springerville (nearest town with a supermarket, 45 miles northwest) with a neighbor for supplies, my first time out to pavement since April. Back home late that afternoon, somewhat dazed from going to town after such a long spell, I thought: A rogue bear in the canyon; *that's too absurd.*

About 8:30 that evening, I was sitting in my room under my one bare 100 watt bulb, reading *Anna Karenina,* when I heard the dogs barking by my full-time neighbors several hundred yards down the canyon. A few min-utes later, I heard a doe that lived around here hooting alarm as she bounded off across the field. I thought: *maybe that's the bear,* but I continued reading, figuring a bear would avoid human presence, especially with the electric light on.

About 8:50, I heard a loud thump behind the windowless northern wall of my room. I picked up my flashlight and looked out through the glass door at the door of the trailer. There, sure enough, stood a very large bear! It knocked the 4x4 aside and pulled the latchless trailer door open, then went in, no doubt looking for food. I had 50 lbs. of whole wheat flour stored in five gallon plastic buckets in the trailer to keep it from raccoons, which once chewed the lid off a bucket stored in the barn. Other staples were in more buckets, jars and cans, a plastic container of honey with my current bottle of cooking oil on the counter. I keep cast-iron pans, which retain food odors, in the closed ice box.

The bear banged around for a while in the trailer, then came back out and went behind it, where it smashed the window over the sink and gashed the screen. I have no idea why—unless maybe out of hungry frustration. Next it climbed into the bed of the pickup, paced back and forth, and threw a can of gasoline out on the other side. Then it walked around the pickup and stood up by the passenger door, the side closest to me. I keep any trash that might have a food smell in the cab of the pickup because it is the most critter proof place I've got. I wash containers with food odors (especially of meat or empty fish cans) so as not to stink up the truck—but also to avoid attracting bears.

Thinking the bear was awfully aggressive to break in with my light on and with me present, shining a flashlight on it, I did not shout at it, afraid of calling its attention to me. Afterwards, I wished I had. It might have saved some damage.

The bear didn't try to break into the truck. Instead, it paced about. Then it walked up to the door of my room.

The bear got about two feet from the door where it finally saw me, standing there the same distance away inside. "Wuff," it said. Which sounded to me like disgust at realizing there was a human being here. Then it turned back between the room and the trailer and moved toward the river to my west. But it must have circled back south, as I later found tracks heading out that way down the driveway.

When I was reasonably confident the bear was gone, I went out and fired up the truck (the first time I'd started it since the registration expired) and drove over to my neighbors. One of them came back with me and we checked things over. I measured a couple of the bear's tracks. They were 9" long by 7" wide. Not an inexperienced yearling, but a large adult.

Other than the smashed window and gashed screen, the most notable damage was done to the frame of a cabinet above the stove. Although it had slid the door open without breaking it, the bear had knocked food containers around but hadn't managed to break anything open. Considering how big and, I presume, hungry the bear was to invade a human habitation with a light on, and how much banging around it did in a 7x12 trailer full of stuff, I thought the amount of damage was remarkably slight.

That night I stayed with neighbors and used their

phone to call Game and Fish in the morning. I felt that a bear that would break into a place where a person was staying, with a light on, was aggressive enough to be dangerous to other people, especially campers. Though it was a Sunday, the G & F officer for this area came up a few hours later. He brought a live trap: a big steel barrel on its own trailer, baited with meat scraps and with a heavy steel drop door. If the bear had come back and he had caught it, he would've had to relocate it some distance away on the border of the National Forest, near the Apache Reservation.

The trap stayed here five days, but the bear never came back. Not surprising really. I suspect that one reason bears and mountain lions have managed to survive as long as they have, with the human population continuing to expand, is because the animals that are left have decided humans are dangerous and that it's best to keep away from us.

Lake In Winter

Fog, pierced by a shaft
of yellow light, curls back
from the lake's edge
to show the banks of snow
slowly drifting.

A skin of ice conceals
the thin surface blackness,
round the rim of the weir
drawing the turgid water in
to swell the surging river.

Revealed, the crystal world
at the lake's arctic center;
the still-life of birds
that summer thrives there,
migrants from another season.

Only quirky lake-fowl stir.
They pick their ginger way
across the ice floes banking
bitter reeds, their ousted home,
stiff and blanched as dried flax.

This is the survival world,
teeth of the earth's famine:
nothing green can grow
ice world, ice kingdom,
its canopy is fog and snow.

—*J.D. Mallinson*

The Hardest Season

By Tom Noyes

SOME PEOPLE IN MANCHESTER and Bennington will tell you there are no black bears left in the Green Mountains, but I know otherwise. Three miles into the maples, oaks and birches behind my house, along the creek that splits my property into two almost perfect halves, I've seen them.

Once from the top of a hill, Jon and I watched a bear waist-deep in the current bob for trout. When it got one, it waded to the bank, sat on the grass, and bit off the head. And in winter, a January afternoon when the sun on the snow glared brighter than the sky, we saw one that should've been sleeping rip the bark off a maple like it was peeling an orange and then chew deeply into the frozen trunk.

There was another time, a steamy, thick-aired July evening that ended a week of rain. The creek was fast and cold and we were fishing without waders, in just shorts and sneakers. It takes a while to catch your breath in water like that, but eventually it feels good. A few times I held my rod over my head and cooled my chest and shoulders by bending my knees to the rocks and mud of the creek bottom.

Jon was at one of his favorite spots, a shady pool under a black, leaning oak, and I was a hundred feet further upstream, out in the open, trying to get a feel for

the fish and what they wanted so I could catch them
before they got to Jon. I was standing, changing flies,
when I spotted the bear thirty yards away on the nearest
bank, a big sow on its haunches eating two-pawed at a
raspberry bush. I slowly made my way to Jon, my rod
held out in front of me for balance. When he looked at
me I pointed.

We stood and watched her. She ripped a section off
the bush, picked it clean, and threw it over her shoulder
like a bone. "She's a big one," Jon said.

"What do you think?" I asked. "We could move
downstream past the bend and be out of her way."

"We could," Jon said, "but this is where the hungry
fish are." He held his rod in one hand and let his other
hand dangle free in the water, downstream from the rest
of him, so it looked like the creek was trying to pull him
back to fishing. "Besides, she looks like a vegetarian."

"She's an omnivore," I said.

"Well, I'm a Methodist." He pulled his line through
his hand until he held his fly between his thumb and fore-
finger. He brought it up to his eyes for inspection, then
dropped it on the water and looked back at the bear.

She saw us at that moment and froze, and we froze,
and nothing other than the creek moved for what seemed
a long time, but then she turned back to her berries, and I
sneezed, and Jon's pole jerked almost out of his hands,
and line was spinning off his reel, and something was run-
ning with his fly.

"I've got one on." Jon raised the tip of his rod,
reeled in some line, then let it down again. The bear

stretched her neck in our direction and aimed her nose higher into the breeze coming off the water. "Big one," he said.

It took Jon a few minutes to reel in close enough to where I could help with the net. What I saw at the end of the line I couldn't believe. There were two trout, small and shiny steel gray, both hooked neatly through the lip. I lifted the line out of the creek and they dangled angrily, kicking each other with their tails. By holding them still with my hand and looking closely, I could tell which one had struck first.

"Not bad," I said. "Haven't seen this trick before."

Jon smiled and nodded toward the bank. The bear had moved to another bush a few feet downstream. "And we have a witness."

We stayed in the creek even after our shadows had stretched long onto the bank. Until the bear left, I checked on her after every few casts. She took occasional, short breaks from the berries and watched us, tilted her neck and spun her head to follow our quick-dipping flies.

Two weeks later there was another bear. Jon and I were working at the time, closing in on the end of a day.

Besides being friends who fished together, Jon and I were business partners. We owned a wood lot, a tractor, a box-frame wagon, and a plow. In the summer we cut and delivered firewood, and in the winter we moved snow.

We saw many of our customers in both seasons, and they appreciated the work we did. In the heat of July and August, they brought us iced tea as we stacked oak and

maple in their garages or on their patios, and in winter,
after we cleared their driveways, some invited us into
their kitchens to take off our gloves and drink coffee. It
was good to look in the living rooms and see logs we'd cut
stacked by the fireplace or stood up, drying against the
wood stove, and it was satisfying driving up and down the
frozen crushed stone driveways, watching the white-gray
smoke ribbon out of chimneys. When it was Jon's turn to
plow, when I was shoveling a walk or unburying a car, I
liked to breathe it in.

Summer in the woods with the trees was the hardest
season. We averaged three cords a day, cut and delivered.
Even though we worked in the shade and it was cooler
there than it must've been haying a field, filling pot holes,
or shingling a roof, it was work that sent us home sore,
and it seemed sometimes to be too much. Still, we liked
it. The smells of sap and sawdust and gasoline and oil
helped keep us awake and fresh, and we liked the system
and order of our work.

After choosing a tree, we opened a triangle low in the
trunk with a chain saw. If it needed help, if it looked like
it might fall back into us or sideways, we stuck wedges in
the gap and hit them with sledge hammers.

A falling tree shakes things up. It scatters birds. It
can't be perfectly planned. It can take smaller trees with
it on its way down, it can catch in a clump of birches, or
it can get snagged in a bigger tree. Sometimes when this
happens, all that's needed is your finger. You touch it
and it's down. Sometimes it takes two men leaning on it.
Other times, after you've already tried touching and lean-

ing and you're standing back thinking of a plan, the wind blows hard enough for something to give, and it crashes, scaring the breath out of you.

When Jon and I had a tree on the ground, one of us took to its crown to zip off the thin, green, leafy branches, and the other marked the trunk with a four-foot measuring stick and red chalk. We then hooked the tree up to the tractor, pulled it to the clearing and cut logs. When we'd gone through enough trees for a cord, we stacked the four foot by eight foot box-frame four foot high and cinched the load down with chains.

On the way to the woods in the mornings, I drove and Jon rode the empty wagon. In the afternoons we switched. Of course, then the wagon was stacked with wood—no room for passengers—so I rode on top of the pile. We had this arrangement because Jon was scared of heights. He lived in a one story house and couldn't get on a ladder to paint the trim or adjust his TV antenna, so I did those things for him, and at the end of a day in the woods I climbed the logs, sat in the middle of the wagon-load for balance, and stretched my legs flat over the thick-linked chain in a wide V. I slipped my hand between the wood and the chain, a bull-rider's grip, and when I was settled, I raised my hand.

If I'd wanted, I probably could've squeezed onto the tractor in the space behind the driver's seat, but that's where we kept the saws, the other tools, and our water jugs, so it would've been tight. Plus I liked to kid Jon. Sometimes he'd look up at me on top of the pile and say, "It doesn't look that high from down here."

"About eight feet," I'd say, and I'd turn to one side and lean my neck and shoulders over the edge, and I'd put my hand over my heart. "But it's a high eight feet."

On the road we sometimes hit a bump or a pot hole and the logs under me would shift. I'd tighten my grip on the chain, find a new spot if I had to, and Jon would turn around and smile and shrug his shoulders. Sometimes while he was doing this, we'd hit another bump, but he never lost a log and I never fell off.

Once, working the first tree of the morning, I hit a knot and my saw kicked back. At first there were just ripped jeans and a white, empty gash above my knee, but then quickly there was blood, even some on my hands and arms. I fell back and yelled. Jon's saw shut off and then he was standing over me.

"My leg," I said. I was breathing fast and holding tightly onto fistfuls of leaves and sticks.

Without speaking, Jon ripped open the tear in my jeans. He looked and inhaled once quickly through his teeth before getting the water jug and flooding the cut. "Try to hold still," he said, and he took off his t-shirt, ripped it lengthwise, and tied it tightly around my leg above the knee. "How's that?"

"Tight," I said.

"Good." He put a hand on my arm. "I don't want to, but I think I'm going to have to leave you here and go get help. It looks like it could be bad and I don't think you're up for a wagon ride." He looked around the clearing and pointed. "Let's get you over to that tree so you can lean back." I nodded without turning to look where he meant. From behind, he grabbed me under the arms and pulled, and I pushed along the ground with my good leg.

When I was set up, back-straight, against an old oak at the edge of the clearing, he carefully raised my leg and rolled a thick log under my calf to keep my knee up. Once I was okay, he found my saw, started it, and let it scream for a few seconds before shutting it off and laying it beside me. My blood was still splattered across the blade.

"Just in case something smells you opened up and thinks about taking a look," he said, "it might not be a bad idea to let her rip once in a while. Keep them honest."

I nodded. "For a second there I thought you wanted me to finish up the rest of the order while you were gone."

"Only if you're feeling up to it." He kneeled and stuck out his hand, and we shook like we were making a deal. "Archie's house is closest. I'll call for help from there. You'll have to sit tight."

"I'm all right," I said. "Just don't stop by Piper's for a beer."

"Don't worry," he said, and he looked at his watch. "Not open yet."

When he showed up an hour later with ambulance volunteers and a stretcher, I was out cold. "Your face was white like cotton," he later told me. "I thought we'd lost you until one of the guys put his ear to your mouth, said you were breathing."

The doctor at the hospital in Bennington said I was lucky. He kept me overnight, but in two weeks I was

back out in the woods, hardly limping, filling orders.
"Another half-inch into your leg with that blade and
there's serious damage," he said.

"That's why I give him the dull saw, Doc," Jon said.
"Otherwise he'd hurt himself."

Procession

Like dolphins, these giant rocks
dive under Cowanshannock's rapids
watch whole trees uproot, nude,
no leaves, no bark,
casketed in solid oak, sycamore, white pine,
float overhead, shouldered on a rising boulder,
one carried high as a sign of respect
for its two hundred years of nurturing
Cowanshannock's wildflowers.
The creek takes care of its own,
bearing the weight of centuries like a single leaf,
no sign of strain, shoulder to shoulder,
carrying its dead to the Allegheny,
providing shelter for its fish,
resurrecting its many lives.

—Ronald F. Smits

It strikes us as fitting that *Tales for the Trail* was crafted in the Catskill Mountains of upstate New York: All of these stories and poems are set in forested, mountainous, or watery terrain, ranging from New York's Adirondacks to California, Colorado, Maine, Montana, North Carolina, Vermont, with other "base camps" along the trail.

In publishing this book in a hand-crafted manner we had two purposes:

One, the cream white, skin-textured paper is good to feel on the tips of those fingers used to turn a page, and therefore should appeal to "armchair adventurers" who prefer reaching for books on their shelves to wandering into weather-whipped, treacherous terrain. Thus, without ever having to climb out of a favorite easy chair, they are able to hike up the rugged crest of a mountain in a lightning storm; or to roar down a wild river in a kayak; or to be buffeted in a light aircraft by a snow squall; or to paddle a wooden canoe from a cove into a lake, revisiting New England history in rhythm with the current.

Two, the vellum which makes up this book is not only a delight to see and touch, but it is also an acid-free, durable stock that is tough enough to satisfy those who insist on actually hauling body and soul up and down forty-six peaks (each between 4,000 and 5,000 feet high) across the Adirondack Mountains; or hiking into a remote river canyon with pack and canteen in California; or flyfishing alongside a black bear in Vermont. In short, this book has been constructed with hardy materials, printed without the assistance of computers, so that one can tuck it into a backpack, if so inclined, as a lively and organic companion on the trail.

Bears show up, uninvited, in three stories herein, and in two cases the blood is stirred but, thankfully, not smeared around. The bears are simply out there, stomping about, exercising ancient rights, and the narrators are smart enough to keep a safe distance. Yet not so great a distance that they can't feel their own blood stirred by the recognition that they share this earth with these existential, essential creatures. In all instances, the participants come away enlarged by the experience. Including, we imagine, the bears.

A number of serious mishaps do occur in the course of these writings, however—a small aircraft, on a solemn mission, crashes near the remote homestead of a dead friend; an exhausted mountain climber, nearing his goal, takes a direct hit by lightning; hikers are washed out by a mountainside torrent; a limb is gnarled by a chain saw in the backwoods. But each of these adventurers emerges from the experience more whole than when they entered into this silent compact with a sometimes harsh nature, and this fact has unexpectedly surfaced as a central theme for this little anthology: When we go into the wilderness, we come out of it as slightly altered, better people.

For this reason, in our opinion, everyone who hikes through a forest, climbs a mountain, paddles a lake—whether by boot or by book—owes it to the earth to speak out on behalf of the land, forest, water, and air of our lives. To achieve a state of adventure calmed by moments of quietude, after all, one must first have mountains, forests, lakes, and fresh air.

—the editors

ABOUT THE AUTHORS

Christopher Boone's finely tuned poem, "glorious mournful," with its crow caws and rotted log, comes to this anthology out of White River Junction and Norwich, Vermont.

Pamela Lee Cranston is an ordained Episcopalian minister in the San Francisco Bay area, but she lost her heart in upstate New York's Adirondack Mountain wilderness, setting for both her Dix Mountain and Giant Mountain pieces.

Ed Ford grew up in Lexington, MA. He graduated from Carleton College, attended the University of Virginia, and the University of Bergen in Norway. His first published book was *Alain-Fournier and Le grand Meaulnes.*

Harry Groome's story in this book, "No Trails to Follow," won the Authors in the Park 2000 Short Story Contest. Another of his stories will appear in a forthcoming Birch Brook Press anthology on flyfishing. Groome fishes, climbs, writes out of Villanova, PA.

Adventurer-veterinarian-novelist *Sid Gustafson* has published fiction in two Birch Brook Press anthologies, *The Suspense of Loneliness* as well as this current book. He tends his "flock" in Bozeman, Montana.

In addition to being a strong poet with publication in various literary magazines, *David Jauss* is a flyfisherman and member of the English Department at the University of Arkansas, Little Rock.

Thomas J. King's delightful essay and poem, "The Rainbow Benediction," comes by way of Citrus Heights, CA, where he dreams of returning to a special canyon that offers many natural delights, including an occasional naked sunbather.

J.D. Mallinson is an educator currently lodged in Laconia, NH. While living in Europe, Mallinson had two volumes published by the University of Salzburg Press, and published poems in leading lit-mags, such as *Contemporary Review*.

Virginia Rudasill Mortenson's kayaking adventure takes place during a camping trip to the wild Nantahala River in North Carolina. But she creates her stories out of Des Moines, Iowa.

Though his inspiration for his poem in this book came from a 'wind song' on a morning in Maine, *David Napolin* writes out of Port Washington, Long Island, New York.

Tom Noyes' fiction has appeared in *American Literary Review, Ascent, High Plains Literary Review, Whetstone*. He has been a member of the creative writing faculty at Indiana State U.

Gordon Frank Rich resides in Canyon Country, California, inspiration for his ode to backpacking in this collection, with its imaginatively expressed concern for overuse of our forests.

Uncle River is a self-proclaimed hermit who has spent the last seven years reading and writing in and around a shack on a friend's unoccupied acreage in the remote Blue River Canyon, NM. Lately he has been searching for a new hermitage.

Poet-essayist *Harry Smith* finds much of his creative inspiration in two diverse locations: Brooklyn and Maine. He is co-founder of the first small press trade association, COSMEP, and is publisher of the legendary lit-mag, *The Smith*.

Ronald F. Smits is professor of English at Indiana University of Pennsylvania and lives in Ford City, PA. His poems have appeared in many journals, including *Southern Review, Pittsburgh Post-Gazette, Texas Observer*.

Roxanne Williams is a novelist, story writer and poet with at least 35 poems published in literary magazines. After a series of life-changing events, she found healing in the redemptive currents of the Colorado River.

DEDICATION

This short book, not likely to ever be atop any best-seller list, is dedicated to all those who know that just having money is not the measure of one's understanding of money. Regardless of the role that Bitcoin ends up playing in our future economy, the underlying principles that govern Bitcoin's rise over the past decade and a half must be understood. The *truth* behind this rise must be understood, so ultimately, this book is dedicated to truth seekers everywhere.

CONTENTS

ACKNOWLEDGMENTS

I am not a financial planner. I carry no recognized certifications that are the hallmark of the traditional financial system. You the reader may very well have more monetary based wealth than I do. My voice as expressed in this book is simply the amalgamation of approximately six years of Bitcoin related study and is only possible because of some very insightful, prescient, and forward-thinking people who now occupy the Bitcoin space. To all of those who saw early on what Bitcoin could become, thank you.

FORWARD

My dear friend and colleague has put a lot of thought into this purposely small book, and so I am honored to have been asked to write the foreword. I am the Founder of CryptoEd, a Portland State University Blockchain Board Member, and a 30 year tech veteran. John is a Naval Academy graduate, former Marine Officer, and a 20 year entrepreneur. We first crossed paths years ago when we were both involved in the Telecom Expense Management (TEM) industry. That we have both gradually migrated towards the crypto industry is not surprising to me, as the space is full of innovation, economic philosophy, and opportunity.

This book, "Bitcoin Is Not Just Money" will provide new insights and opportunities in the financial and Bitcoin domains. It is hoped that the reader will begin to comprehend Bitcoin and its numerous aspects related to financial principles and how it will open up entirely new business options and opportunities.

Within the domain of financial planning or portfolio management, Bitcoin has historically been regarded as a high risk asset to be ignored. It now appears poised to be recognized as at least a medium of exchange but also as a groundbreaking asset with numerous applications. As such, it represents a paradigm shift in the financial environment, altering the concepts of investment, security, hedging, and decentralization, even beyond its monetary worth.

Financial specialists are beginning to see beyond market swings to comprehend Bitcoin and its peer-to-peer mobility. Comprehending its technological foundation, known as the blockchain, is crucial. The foundation of Bitcoin as a decentralized ledger that promotes security, immutability, and transparency while offering novel solutions that go beyond established financial institutions, is almost impossible to completely comprehend.

Additionally, Bitcoin challenges traditional portfolio

diversification tactics as a new asset class. Because of its restricted supply, similar scarcity to precious metals, and distinctive qualities, it presents opportunities and hazards that call for a careful approach when integrating it into traditional investment portfolios.

Beyond just being profitable, Bitcoin represents a philosophical position on financial sovereignty. Financial inclusion is promoted by giving individuals authority over their wealth, irrespective of geographical restrictions and middlemen.

But this revolutionary potential also entails volatility and regulatory uncertainty, necessitating caution and a well-informed approach. Hence, in order to effectively navigate the Bitcoin arena, financial specialists need to arm themselves with extensive knowledge, stay up to date on technical and regulatory developments, and use tools to reduce risks for their clients.

For professionals in the financial industry, Bitcoin is significant not only for its value as money but also because it represents empowerment, innovation, and the changing face of finance. It makes a case for a comprehensive review of conventional wisdom, pushing financial advisors to acknowledge how wealth and technology are changing.

My belief in this project of John's is such that in addition to writing this Forward, we collaborated on a final chapter that delves into the tax implications of cryptocurrencies, which is an ever changing regulatory hurdle that wealth managers will need to be aware of. While neither John nor I claim to be the definitive source for anything crypto, it is my hope that this book will help pave the way for a whole new wave of interest on the part of those who have been entrusted with the financial future of others.

Tanya Seda   January 2024   Tucson, AZ

INTRODUCTION

Many years ago, while the CEO of a small technology company, I was looking for warehouse space with a real estate agent who brought me, along with my brother, to a location in the small town of Purvis, MS. This facility was about 10 miles south of our company's location in Hattiesburg, MS and the rental rates were presumably a bit better than what we could find closer to home.

Our company was in need of warehouse space because we were on the short list of vendors vying for a contract with the city of Philadelphia school system. If we were awarded the contract, we were going to be setting up or "kitting" the tablets for all of their students, and we simply didn't have the space for such an undertaking at our main office.

Upon entering the facility, one immediately heard a soft "hum" or "buzz" coming from the other side of the facility. The agent explained that the humming was coming from hundreds, or possibly thousands of computers that were doing some weird thing with "magic Internet money." He didn't really understand much about the process, but as far as he knew, these computers stayed on all the time, and the owners of all the computers somehow got paid with Internet tokens for the trouble of running all these computers.

As sourcing tablets for Philadelphia school students seemed much more lucrative to me at the time than some sort of magic Internet money, I ignored the noise, and gave it very little thought in the short term. As it turned out, the sales rep we had hired to go after these large type of accounts was himself, a scam. While he said all the right things, I don't actually believe we were ever truly in contention for the contract. I mention this here not to cause slander, but simply to point out the irony of that day: I thought the computer money that was being "mined" was a complete hoax, a complete scam. Instead, I was being scammed by a sales rep who had led me to believe that we were a few short steps away from a highly lucrative, and company changing contract.

For those who have paid any attention to the crypto space over the past few years, it is perhaps obvious that scams are perhaps a bit more frequent than in traditional finance. As an advocate for the crypto space, I certainly hate that this is true. I myself have not been immune to some of these problems that have plagued the space. Sam Bankman-Fried and his FTX exchange never seemed right to me, so I was never sucked into his orbit, but I did lose money with a project called Terra Luna and the stablecoin used on its network called UST. This was particularly painful, because I had moved into this stablecoin because it was like a digital dollar, but in this case, an algorithmically backed token that was supposed to always maintain its peg to the US dollar. In other words, this was my "safe" play while the broader markets were headed down. I was thinking I was really a brilliant investor because I'd largely gotten out of Bitcoin and was now in something safer, ready to get back in when the markets turned bullish again.

I mention one of my own mistakes early on because on some level, I think it's a bit of a badge of honor. If you can find a crypto savant or sherpa to guide you through this space who has no scars, I'd question their worth. This space is still quite young. It can at times be an emotional grind, especially for those who only view it in terms of price action. It has attracted a wild assortment of characters, from anarchists to alchemists, from believers to deceivers. The cast of characters who call crypto home are difficult to categorize, with the best of them envisioning entirely new and equitable financial systems while the worst see nothing but quick profits.

In order to figure out just where you might potentially fit in within this participatory spectrum, this short work begins with a short discussion of economic theory. It is not an all encompassing overview of financial or investment practices, but rather, seeks to help you more accurately assess the theories or foundations that underlie your current practice.

Having presumably established an investment philosophy, or gained a bit more focus regarding your philosophy, the next three chapters are focused on Bitcoin as something other than money. In Chapter 2, I'll discuss it as a protocol, in Chapter 3, I'll compare it to a tech stock, and in Chapter 4, I'll examine it as a pure hedging mechanism. Chapter 5 will consider Bitcoin as a proverbial lifeboat in troubled times while Chapter 6 will examine a bit of Bitcoin's history so as to get a meaningful sense as to where it is right now in its adoption cycle.

My crypto-collegue, Tanya Seda has rightfully recommended a short chapter regarding taxes. While this is not a topic many "crypto-curious" people want to really explore, it is important to at least get a sense of the issue. Finally, Chapter 8 represents an addition to the original version, something that became necessary in light of the Trump Administration's creation of a Bitcoin Strategic Reserve.

In my time studying Bitcoin specifically and the broader crypto space in general, there have been numerous sources that have had major impacts on me. This book is in many ways a reflection of those sources, though they have been amalgamated and repurposed into something I hope is of value. I have set out to write this book over the course of one week, and have in fact given myself a strict deadline in which to achieve this. In no way is this a "magnum opus," or the definitive guide to cryptocurrencies. Rather, I am just more and more convinced that Bitcoin's potential role in our world is changing, or is at least up for debate. In order for something truly profound to come out of this debate, it will be necessary for people from all backgrounds to have insight as to its possibilities and even its pitfalls.

For readers who have begun experimenting or implementing AI applications, you will perhaps know that "generative" AI can be a rather quick and even fun way to gain meaning or make sense from various source materials very quickly. In some ways, I'm trying to do something similar, by taking much of the material I have read or listened to over the past six years and trying to succinctly repackage it in a way that makes sense for those who have the responsibility of managing money (theirs or that of others).

Rather than simply providing references as they appear in this short work, I provide here some of the voices in this space who have been fundamental in my understanding of this ever changing domain:

Saifedean Ammous: economist, author, podcaster. Published works I have read:
The Bitcoin Standard

Ammous has produced what is in some ways a trilogy of books related to monetary systems and the possible role of Bitcoin in the future. His latest two books, *The Fiat Standard* and *The Principles of Economics* complement *The*

Bitcoin Standard, and for many within the Bitcoin space, these books represent something close to seminal reading.

Andreas Antonopoulos: technologist, entrepreneur, and educator. Certainly one of the kindest human beings in the sometimes toxic world of cryptocurrencies. Published works I have read:
Mastering Bitcoin: Unlocking Digital Cryptocurrencies

Antonopoulos on YouTube is a treasure trove of information focused on Bitcoin. He is part of the Crypto Currency Certification Consortium (C4) and continues to put out educational content across a variety of mediums.

Vijay Boyapati: moved to the US from Australia in the early 2000's in order to pursue a PhD in computer science. He ended up at a small start up called Google instead. He Left Google in '07 to help raise money for Ron Paul's presidential campaign. Published works I have read: *The Bullish Case for Bitcoin.*

Boyapati's book is in many ways a synthesis of essays and other writings related to money, and the rise of Bitcoin. Somewhat similar to Ammous, Boyapati provides a great deal of monetary history in his attempt to show why Bitcoin is already showing the traits of hard money.

Robert Breedlove: a "freedom maximalist" and former hedge fund manager, he has become well respected for his philosophical vantage point by which he continues to explore money and Bitcoin. His podcast episode "The

Number Zero and Bitcoin" is a fascinating look at the seemingly mundane concept of a "space holder."

Caitlen Long: formerly of Goldman Sachs, now CEO of Custodia Bank. Long is a resident of Wyoming and is helping make it the "Delaware of Cryptocurrency." Long is closely allied with Wyoming Senator Cynthia Lummis who is widely acknowledged as one of the biggest supporters of Bitcoin in Washington, DC.

Michael Saylor: former CEO of MicroStrategy, the first publicly traded company to use Bitcoin as its reserve asset. He is also the founder of the non-profit Saylor Academy which provides free courses and certifications across a wide array of subjects. Saylor is in many ways the godfather of Bitcoin and is quite public about his view that there is Bitcoin, and then there is everything else.

In addition to these Bitcoin "voices" mentioned above, there is a current underlying my entire understanding, or vision of this space that originated in my reading *The Sovereign Individual.* This book, with the subtitle, "Mastering the Transition to the Information Age," was first published in 1997. Written by James Dale Davidson and Lord William Rees-Mogg, I came to read this book largely because of the 2020 edition that includes a Preface by venture capitalist Peter Thiel. The lines that most captured my attention:

"In truth, the great conflict over our megapolitical future is only just beginning. On the dimension of technology, the conflict has two poles: AI and crypto. Artificial Intelligence holds out the prospect

of finally solving what economists call the "calculation problem": AI could theoretically make it possible to centrally control an entire economy. It is not coincidence that AI is the favorite technology of the Communist Party of China. Strong cryptography, at the other pole, holds out the prospect of a decentralized and individualized world. If AI is communist, crypto is libertarian."

When I first read that book, I was still early in my study of crypto. The idea that "crypto is libertarian," and represents the polar opposite of authoritarian China in many ways served as something of a "greenlight" for me to continue exploring the space. Why would I need "permission?"

First off, I'm a graduate of the US Naval Academy (class of 1998). I was a Marine Corps Infantry Officer. I was born, raised, and remain a Roman Catholic. Those facts alone imply that I like order and am comfortable with hierarchy. While I'm perhaps not always thrilled with the current hierarchical structure in place, I expect it. Dogmas and doctrine do not represent handcuffs to me, rather they often represent deep thinking that has percolated into accepted truths.

I mention the above, because on the surface, I am at the bottom of the list when it comes to people "most likely to get into crypto." I say "on the surface," because when I critically examine my own past, things start to make a bit more sense. For example, while at the Academy, I played baseball for a coach who was incredibly dogmatic. My approach to hitting was different than his. He viewed my difference as defiance, and for that, I was perpetually in his doghouse. He would eventually lose his job in Annapolis, though I wonder to this day if he ever figured out that his inability to connect with most of his players was due to his inability to distinguish dogma from personal preference.

As an Economics major studying at the time of the Internet's emergence, I was almost at ground zero in terms of accepted classical economic principles and a seemingly unlimited array of commercial and military possibilities for those willing to think creatively.

It was in school that I first discovered that the term "money supply" was actually composed of some assortment of different monetary instruments, and that economists had given unique identifiers to these classifications:

M0: the strictest, smallest measure of the money supply, it is the money in general circulation plus commercial bank reserves held at the Federal Reserve.

M1: all the notes and coins in circulation, sometimes called the "narrow" supply, it can be thought of as the most liquid category.

M2: includes everything in M1, but also includes short term bank deposits and individual money market funds.

M3: included everything in M1 and M2 with the addition of institutional deposits and money market funds (as of 2006, this was deemed to difficult to track, so has been largely discontinued, at least officially.

For the novice (me), learning the above was almost groundbreaking. I had always been under the impression that money was money. Sure, I had a grasp of things like currency conversion to take into account the monies of different countries, but the idea that within the confines of a nation, there were definitive, and quantitative differences amongst "types" of money was a completely new concept.

On the whole, I was an average student at the Naval Academy. Within my chosen major, I was probably right in the middle of the bell curve. I struggled with economic statistics, enjoyed the economics of developing nations, but on the whole, it seemed the entire discipline, or at least the version of it that I was taught, was already settled. I got very little economic theory. I don't recall debates surrounding Keynes or Friedman, but rather, just some general acceptance of theories, terms, and concepts that most of us Midshipmen just accepted as facts.

One of these concepts that I remember first encountering was "GDP" or Gross Domestic Product. My Macroeconomics professor was an Academy graduate himself and had done graduate studies at Wharton while still in the Navy. I don't remember much more about him, but I know that it seemingly took an entire class period for him to explain exactly what all was comprised in this almost Biblical like indicator of economic health.

I never thought about it at the time, but it should strike any market observer as strange that this number isn't called "Gross Domestic Production." The fact that we use the word "Product" is certainly strange, seeing that the number is supposed to assess our nation's ability to make things. I can still see my professor with some degree of clarity writing:

$$GDP = C + I + G + (Exports - Imports)$$

Where "C" is Consumption, "I" is Investment, and "G" is Government

What I do not recall learning in that class, was exactly what percentage of the total GDP figure was coming from Consumption. Based on economic data easily found from the Federal Reserve, consumption currently comprises approximately 68% of GDP, having steadily risen from approximately 58% in the mid 1960's.

Personally, I think this is a really big deal, as the accepted metric by which an administration or central planner points to in order to claim economic growth is a number that is so weighted to consumption, that it becomes clear that we're not "philosophically" a consumer based economy, we are a consumer based economy in reality. So the next time a relatively new household appliance of yours breaks and must be replaced, just remember, your government leaders are excitedly adding that purchase to our nation's GDP.

It was not until I discovered Ludwig Von Mises, roughly 5 years after graduating, that I became a bit more versed in the highly nuanced debates surrounding economic thought. I encountered an Italian economist, diplomat, and politician named Amintore Fanfani. He, perhaps more than any other thinker, forced me into a real dilemma, as one of his main tenants was that Capitalism and Communism ultimately end up morphing into each other. Say what!?!

For a young Marine officer at the time, this put me on some shaky ground, but also gave some freedom to begin thinking more seriously about some of the systems that had simply been accepted over time: dollar as world reserve currency, primacy of the Fed over interest rates, etc.

Some of my personal story is mentioned here in the hopes that it will compel you to re-examine your own story. How do you think of money? How do you distinguish money from wealth? How do you view your role as someone who is supposed to make sense of a world that is clearly changing? What sort of clients do you currently serve? What sort of clients would you like to serve in the future?

Regardless of your own personal story as it pertains to economics and finance, one story you are perhaps familiar with is that of the Dutch tulip bubble. This event, which occurred during the 17th century, is often sited as a cautionary tale as to what can happen when speculation runs amok within markets. Throw in a little "group think" and the desire to get rich quick, and the tulip mania makes sense. Many educated investors start pointing to Dutch tulips in order to dismiss Bitcoin. Not only is this not fair to Bitcoin, it is actually not fair to tulips.

There are several aspects of the tulip craze that often get overlooked or ignored altogether. For example, tulips first came to Holland via the Ottoman Empire sometime in the 16th century. They became popular over several decades, not simply over several years, with the tiny country developing a genuine appetite for rare and exotic varieties. The striking red and white petals of the *Semper Augustus* made it one of the most sought after varieties.

In time, tulip prices began being tracked on various indices and there was in fact a futures market with contracts issued that were tied to the future price. In 1637, when the bubble did in fact burst, it did lead to a short term financial downturn that affected more than just the affected speculators, but the economy rebounded rather quickly, and today, Holland is major producer and exporter of tulips, with this proud plant having a major place in Dutch horticulture in particular and in Dutch culture more generally.

The events that actually caused the Dutch tulip bubble to burst are not widely understood or agreed upon. There are theories that identify the city of Harleem as the auction site that first balked at the seemingly ever increasing prices. Perhaps reality struck those residents first, or perhaps the Harleem theory carries no weight. Regardless of which auction site failed to produce the speculative buyers that had previously fueled the rising prices, the ensuing collapse did bring regulations and government intervention in an early quest to prevent financial uncertainty.

	Tulips	Bitcoin	Gold
Aesthetically Pleasing?	Yes	No	Yes
Traded on a Futures Market?	Yes	Yes	Yes
Global Marketplace?	Yes	Yes	Yes
Historical Track Record of Being Money or a Store of Value?	Yes	No	Yes
Material Amounts Can Be Taken Across Borders in Time of Crisis?	No	Yes	No

What hopefully stands out in this chart is that at least in this very limited look, gold has more in common with tulips than does Bitcoin. The aesthetically pleasing aspects of both gold and tulips are undeniable, as is the fact that both have track records of being highly valuable.

While tulips don't sit in central bank vaults in the way that gold does, there continues to be great global appreciation for them. As Forbe's Senior Contributor Cecila Rodriguez notes, one of the things that really adds to their appeal, is they "lack the connotations of romance or grief attached to other flowers." Because tulips seem to stand on their own, many observers believe the tulip may have passed up the rose as the world's most popular flower.[1]

That a study of Bitcoin would include a short nod to the world of horticulture might strike some as strange, but it is done with a genuine purpose: economic bubbles are not new, nor do they indicate a problem with the asset that is being unnaturally inflated. When the housing bubble burst in 2008, very few people began bemoaning the existence of houses. Instead, a great many US residents simply became familiar with the term "sub-prime mortgages."

As 2023 comes to a close, many believe that housing has again reached bubble bursting stage. I am assuming that houses will still be looked upon favorably should a collapse ensue.

The aim of this book is not to convince you to immediately open up a Coinbase or Kraken account and begin investing or trading in Bitcoin. The aim is however to get you thinking about it in ways that you have not previously. You may choose to join the ranks of Charlie Munger and Warren Buffett who have quite

---

[1] https://www.forbes.com/sites/ceciliarodriguez/2023/04/16/tulip-mania-and-the-multimilliondollar-industry-behind-the-worlds-popular-flower/?sh=19bed0ed37d9

publicly expressed their disdain for cryptocurrencies, and that is fine. What is not fine, is for those with a fiduciary responsibility to their clients, to dismiss it simply because it is not understood. Whether you love Bitcoin or hate it, it should be for a good reason, not because you haven't taken the time to actually try and grasp it.

From January of '23 to December of '23, Bitcoin has risen from about $16,579 to approximately $40,760. If you are a financial planner without a mandate to grow your clients wealth, or to at least preserve it, these numbers may mean very little to you. For those keeping score though, these numbers represent a 145.85 percentage increase over the most recent twelve months. To be fair, Bitcoin had been pummeled in the preceding two years, so some observers might cynically think it simply had more to rise than other assets. There would be an element of truth to that, but it seems logical to also assert that a more important reality is that Bitcoin simply doesn't seem to go away. It has been declared "dead" by so many pundits that its very existence today must account for something, and I would assert, it is the fact that it continues to exist in such a hostile environment that it is worthy of your study.

1
YOUR INVESTMENT PHILOSOPHY

"The stock market is filled with individuals who know the price of everything, but the value of nothing."

~ Phillip Fisher

Regardless of the size of your practice, if you have achieved any level of success or longevity, it is likely that you have managed to express to the market in some way that you have an "edge" or a philosophy that resonates with some portion of the market you have set out to serve.

Modern Portfolio Theory (MPT) is potentially one of the frameworks you have adopted, or perhaps adapted to your personal style. Developed by economist Harry Markowitz in the 1950s, it aims to maximize the expected return of a portfolio for a given level of risk or minimize the risk for a given level of expected return. Some of the key principles of Modern Portfolio Theory include:

Diversification: MPT emphasizes the importance of diversifying investments to reduce risk. By spreading investments across different asset classes (such as stocks, bonds, and other securities) that are not perfectly correlated, the overall portfolio risk can be mitigated.

Risk and Return: MPT recognizes that there is a trade-off between risk and return. Investors should be compensated for taking on higher levels of risk with the expectation of higher returns. The goal is to achieve the optimal balance between risk and return for a given investor's risk tolerance.

Efficient Frontier: The efficient frontier is a concept

in MPT that represents the set of portfolios that offer the maximum expected return for a given level of risk or the minimum risk for a given level of expected return. Portfolios on the efficient frontier are considered optimal because they provide the best risk-return trade-off.

Expected Return and Standard Deviation: MPT uses statistical measures such as expected return and standard deviation to quantify the historical performance and risk of individual assets. These measures are then used to calculate the expected return and risk of a portfolio based on the weights assigned to each asset.

Correlation: The correlation between assets is crucial in MPT. Assets that are not perfectly correlated provide the benefits of diversification, as they may respond differently to market conditions. Low or negative correlations between assets help to reduce overall portfolio risk.

Capital Market Line (CML): The Capital Market Line is a line that represents the relationship between risk and return for a risk-free investment combined with a risky portfolio. It helps investors understand the trade-off between risk-free assets and risky portfolios.

One of the economic frameworks or "schools" that has been open to the acceptance of Bitcoin has been the Austrian. Unlike Modern Portfolio Theory, the Austrians don't necessarily have a single founder, though Carl Menger (1840–1921) is often given that title. His seminal work, *Principles of Economics*, published in 1871, emphasized the role of individual preference in determining economic value. In other words, the idea of "subjectivity" is at the bedrock of Austrian economics.

Others who built upon Menger include Eugen von Böhm-Bawerk (1851–1914), who is highly regarded for his work pertaining to the importance of time preference. Ludwig von Mises (1881–1973) published *Human Action* in 1949 in which he integrated economics into a broader social science framework. Friedrich Hayek (1899–1992) was a Nobel laureate whose ideas on the limitations of central planning were articulated in his book *The Road to Serfdom* (1944) which is largely considered a classic in political economic theory. Finally, Murray Rothbard (1926–1995) made significant contributions to Austrian Economics, particularly in the areas of economic theory, ethics, and political philosophy. His work *Man, Economy, and State* (1962) is a comprehensive treatise on Austrian economic thought.

While there is something of a clear line of thinking amongst the Austrians, it is worth noting that they don't really have a set of rigid doctrines, which makes sense, for they deplore centralized authorities. For those not familiar with Austrian Economics, but wanting to get a framework, it is worth knowing that in large part, there is a shared emphasis on subjectivism, methodological individualism, and of course, the shared doubt with regards to the effectiveness of central planners.

To imply that the Austrian school and MPT are polar opposites would be erroneous, and not particularly helpful. In fact, a simple ChatGPT search of "Alternatives to Modern Portfolio Theory" doesn't even include Austrian Economics, but rather, generates the following:

1. Post-Modern Portfolio Theory: a bit more nuanced than the original PMT, it uses a bit more statistical analysis.
2. Behavioral Finance: takes into account emotions and cognitive biases.
3. Risk Parity: seeks to diffuse the risk among any

single asset class.

4. Factor Investing: seeks to exploit persistent or known factors that objectively drive returns.
5. Dynamic Asset Allocation: acknowledges that market conditions change over time and that portfolios should be adjusted in response to those changes.
6. Black-Litterman Model: incorporates investor views or sentiment into portfolio construction.
7. Minimum Variance Portfolio: this approach seeks to find an optimal balance of risk and reward, but focuses on risk reduction.
8. Alternative Investments: calls for diversification beyond stocks and bonds, as there is an emphasis on non-correlated returns.

My pitting the Austrian School against Modern Portfolio Theory is not in order to create some sort of binary study of these outlooks. Rather, it is to drive home the fact that you as a trusted advisor do in fact have an investment framework, whether or not you've attempted to articulate it or not. Perhaps your practice began because friends and family felt you were always "good with money," and you never needed a baseline theory in order to get started. Perhaps you are Ivy League educated with an advanced degree in Finance but you have found that your experience as an investor doesn't match up with what you were originally taught. Regardless of where you might fall on the spectrum, one thing is true: your clients think you know something they don't.

Some readers might be familiar with the personality test known as the "Meyers-Briggs Type Indicator." I have no intention of putting you through any sort of formal, economic self-assessment, but it is sometimes helpful to get some clarification on our thought processes, or some confirmation of why we think certain things.

Austrians	Modern Portfolio Theory
Tend towards subjectivity (individual choices and preferences).	Tend towards objectivity (mathematical or statistical analysis).
Acknowledges an outsized impact of entrepreneurial action and activity that drives market activity and potential returns.	Adheres to the Efficient Market Theory and assumes that it is difficult to outperform the market.
Highly skeptical of government intervention and in fact views government intervention is a key driver in mal-investment.	Sees government intervention as part of the efficient working of the markets.

In my own trek down the Bitcoin rabbit hole, I found myself largely reading or listening to those who could typically be labeled as Austrians. This was quite logical, as Bitcoin was the first "decentralized" currency the world had ever seen. In fact, it is this decentralized aspect of Bitcoin that really represents the "invention" that is Bitcoin. Some detractors have rightly pointed out that PayPal or Venmo already provide us the means by which to move money efficiently. What they miss is that such platforms require a middle-man, whereas Bitcoin does not.

The point of this chapter is not to delve into the properties surrounding Bitcoin, but rather, to make this point:

Whether you are an Austrian Economist or a proponent of some form of Modern Portfolio Theory, Bitcoin fits your thesis.

Can this be true? Can two schools of thought that are largely opposed to one another really find common ground around a digital asset that didn't even exist until recently? My assertion is of course in the affirmative, and stems from the idea that the Austrian's doubt regarding the effectiveness of government intervention, along with MPT's belief in the overall efficiency of markets, find true overlap with Bitcoin's known protocol that allows for only 21 million Bitcoin to ever be created.

It is this inflationary "governor switch" that is often the first thing most Bitcoin advocates come to discover or appreciate. This is somewhat obvious in an era of cheap money, low interest rates, and palpably high inflation. For many, this finite amount of Bitcoin makes its comparison to gold quite obvious, as the latter is clearly difficult to mine, and therefore has a very high "stock to flow" ratio (known supply does not change much with the annualized new gold that gets mined).

For the retail investor, this "anti-inflation" narrative is often enough to pique interest, or to at least allocate some safe amount of money to Bitcoin, especially if one's time horizon is long enough. As it pertains to the institutional investor though, or those with a fiduciary duty to clients, to allocate some portion of a portfolio to Bitcoin based on its finite supply is to stop well short of what Bitcoin actually is, and is to make the mistake of seeing Bitcoin as nothing more than a digital hedge against central bank induced inflation.

How you view Bitcoin's future has everything to do with your past, but here's where things get a bit difficult according to James Dale Davidson and Lord William Rees-Mogg. Speaking of the "Merchant Republics of Cyberspace," they contend that it "will therefore be crucial that you see the world anew. That means looking from the outside in to reanalyze much that you have probably taken for granted. This will enable you to come to a new understanding. If you fail to transcend conventional thinking at a time when conventional thinking is losing touch with reality, then you will be more likely to fall prey to an epidemic of disorientation that lies ahead. Disorientation breeds mistake that could threaten your business, your investments, and your way of life."[2]

Sure, it has become a bit trite to talk about "thinking outside the box," but it would appear that many of the events that Davidson and Rees-Mogg were predicting back in 1997 have indeed come true, and so roughly 25 years since they published *The Sovereign Individual,* it serves as something of a baseline for this book, and perhaps a wake up call for you, the Bitcoin hesitant, the crypto skeptic, or the cyber denier.

Since 25 years have passed since the original publication, there has been ample time to evaluate the predictive powers of the authors, so what did these guys get right, and what did they get wrong?

First off, the book is right at 400 pages in length, so it speaks far more in grand themes than in simple

---

[2] Davidson, James Dale and Rees-Mogg, William. The Sovereign Individual. New York: Touchstone, an Imprint of Simon & Schuster, Inc, 2020.

predictions, but very broadly, the authors proposed some version of the following ideas:

- Economic power would shift from labor to capital, with the Internet ushering in an entirely new era of entrepreneurship and creativity.
- Traditional nation states would be challenged by non-nation states in the creation of money and financial systems. Advances in cryptography would allow for the creation of digital currencies.
- Individuals would take greater and greater control of their financial futures.
- The coercive powers of the large nation states would be diminished, and as state sponsored war or violence decreased, lower level crime will increase.

In regards to the first point, the shift from capital to labor can be seen in the manner in which "being able to think of the thing is more important than being able to make the thing." We see this everywhere, and we now know it almost intuitively: entrepreneurs aren't building huge factories where they can manufacture equipment, they're building software that scales so as to deploy it globally.

We know the truth of the second point by the very existence of Bitcoin and all the cryptocurrencies created since Bitcoin's emergence. In regards to the third point, we see Robinhood apps and institutional grade trading software getting more advanced. Gone are the days of financial planners playing the role of gateway into the markets.

This last point regarding the coercive power of the large nation state is still very much playing out in real time, and might be difficult to label as a "correct" prediction. At present, most casual observers would perhaps contend that the coercive powers of the state have never been greater. From COVID lockdowns to entitlement payments that come from a seemingly bottomless treasury, the state seems all powerful right now, but this all hinges on a profound sense of trust permeating the entire system. That trust is crumbling, and with it, so does the government's coercive power.

2

BITCOIN AS A PROTOCOL

"The best protocols are layered, with each layer building on the services provided by the layer beneath it."

~Robert E. Kahn, co-creator of the TCP/IP Protocols

In layman's terms, the practice of using e-mail can be said to consist of three main layers:

1. User Agents. This top layer is essentially the e-mail client used by the end user, and includes well known providers like Microsoft Outlook and Gmail. Within this layer, there are two main access protocols that have risen to the level of a standard: IMAP (Internet Message Access Protocol) or POP3 (Post Office Protocol Version 3). With regards to sending messages, that is done via SMTP (Simple Mail Transfer Protocol).
2. Mail Transfer Agents. This middle layer is where e-mails are routed and transferred (something like a switching station). Here again, SMTP is the primary standard and the utilization of the DNS (Domain Name System) allows for e-mails to make their way to the desired destination.
3. Mail Delivery Agent. This bottom layer is responsible for storage of messages, and again, the IMAP or POP3 standards dictate whether messages are stored locally or on a remote server.

Whether you are familiar with these protocols or layers, you are familiar with e-mail, and you know that it doesn't matter whether you use Gmail and your sister uses

Outloook.   The two of you can communicate quite seamlessly while being on different platforms because the underlying technology utilizes standard protocols.

Of course, e-mail is not the only technology that rests upon similarly accepted standards. Cellphone usage easily comes to mind, though it wasn't always as seamless as it appears to today.   In the early days of cellular adoption, there were plenty of "friends and family" promotions that sought to drive network adoption within a particular carrier's footprint.   Over the past several years, with data becoming more and more a part of the cellular use case, there has been a major push towards 5G, a lower latency standard that is capable of supporting the ever growing demand for data.

As the technologies behind wireless usage have expanded, the standards that support such usage have consolidated.   Gone are the days of limiting your call patterns to nights and weekends. While some degree of data regulation does exist today, it is clear that will not be the case for much longer, after all, new advances in AI need your data, so data will certainly continue to get cheaper so as to feed the thirst for AI and machine learning.

From e-mail usage to cell phones and now even to Zoom calls, one thing is quite clear: when you have established protocols, builders and entrepreneurs can create. Scale can be achieved. Standards allow end users an array of choices, and setting up a phone call or holding a virtual meeting requires only agreeing upon the time and day, not the platform. No one cares who your wireless carrier is.

This examination of standards and protocols might seem out of place in a book centered around financial management, so here's the spin: none of the protocols mentioned above represent anything that someone could have ever invested in. There is no stock ticker "POP3." There are no Bloomberg terminals where you will find information regarding "IMAP" or "SMTP." In short, the only way for investors to have ever made a return on these protocols is to have invested in companies that built products on top of these protocol layers. Bitcoin represents an opportunity to invest in the base layer, and in and of itself, that is incredibly unique.

If instead of thinking about Bitcoin as money, it was thought of as a protocol, what could it then be compared to? The most logical comparison seems to be with the SWIFT system, which employs a closed, secure network that financial institutions use to exchange messages and information. In many ways, it is the "social network" for financial institutions and can loosely be viewed as being composed of or described as:

1. Network Protocol
2. Message Standard
3. Security Measures
4. Global Reach
5. Standards Development

While SWIFT is not necessarily a communication protocol in the technical sense, it is helpful in this study to view it as such. Its standard messaging protocol must be adhered to by users of the system, and has evolved a bit over time. At present, the following components make up a message:

1. Message Type (MT). The message type indicates the purpose or category of the message. For example, MT103 is commonly used for

international wire transfers, while MT202 is used for bank-to-bank transactions.

2. Basic Header (Block 1). Contains information such as the Message Type (MT), the sender's and receiver's SWIFT/BIC (Business Identifier Code) addresses, and the date and time of the message.

3. Application Header (Block 2). Includes information related to the specific application of the message, such as the service identifier and the logical terminal address.

4. User Header (Block 3). Optional block that allows users to include additional information relevant to the transaction.

5. Text Block (Block 4). Contains the main body of the message, including details about the financial transaction. The structure and content of this block depend on the specific message type.

6. Trailer (Block 5). Contains a trailer sequence and optional trailer text. It helps ensure the integrity of the message during transmission.

In many respects, it was the language within the SWIFT messaging system that first got me thinking about Bitcoin and SWIFT. The use of "headers" and "blocks" were quite obvious, and so it becomes pertinent to begin exploring what the criteria behind a valid Bitcoin transaction looks like. The technical details underpinning Bitcoin is not the purpose of this work, but since every node within the network is having to show "Proof of Work" (PoW) it is worth looking at what this "work" involves.

In many respects, Bitcoin is something of a broadcast system, in that each node within the network, upon receiving a transaction, must validate it before pushing it out to its neighbors. This checklist of items can be modified or altered should network participants agree that changes are appropriate.

1. Syntax and Structure. Node must ensure that the transaction adheres to the correct syntax and structure specified by the Bitcoin protocol.
2. Transaction Version. Node must ensure that the transaction version is supported and follows the current protocol rules.
3. Inputs. Node must confirm that each input refers to an unspent transaction output (UTXO) from a previous transaction.
4. Signature Verification. Node must ensure the digital signatures associated with each input to ensure they are correct and match the public keys.
5. Script Evaluation. Node must execute the script associated with each input and ensure that it evaluates to true. This involves checking the locking and unlocking scripts.
6. Transaction Fee. Node must ensure that the transaction includes a sufficient transaction fee to incentivize miners to include it in a block.   trans
7. Double Spending Prevention. Node must ensure that the inputs are not being used in multiple transactions simultaneously, preventing double spending.
8. Output Values. Node must ensure that the sum of output values does not exceed the sum of input values as this ensures that no new bitcoins are created.
9. Locktime. Node must check the locktime field to ensure that the transaction is valid based on the specified time or "block height," which simply

refers to the current block in the blockchain.
10. Ensure the transaction does not contain any non-standard scripts or features that may violate protocol rules and that size block size limits are adhered to.

One of the reasons for showing this modified list of valid transaction criteria is to emphasize that nodes within the Bitcoin network are in fact "working." Many Bitcoin detractors like to assert that there is nothing backing Bitcoin. What they are really asserting is that there is no government funded military backing it. In that, they would be correct, but this chapter is still focused on Bitcoin as a protocol, and so I remain fixed on two truths about Bitcoin from the perspective of it being a protocol, and not just money:

1. It represents the first technological *standard* that one could ever invest in.
2. As a protocol, it is similar to other technologies in that it is open source and can easily be built upon.

As the base layer upon which other applications can be built, there is another crypto currency that financial professionals should be aware of: Ethereum. This crypto emerged in some ways out of the frustration that some developers had with working with the Bitcoin protocol. Within the crypto community, there is an ever raging debate on how to most effectively deal with the "trilemma" that exists within blockchain applications. These are:

1. Security
2. Scalability
3. Decentralization

Striking the right balance amongst these three attributes becomes a challenge that often can't be solved in a way that answers every problem. For example, when a protocol places an emphasis on security, it is quite logical that scalability will suffer. Etheruem emerged in response to developers who believed that Bitcoin's emphasis on security would never allow it to scale in a meaningful way. To some degree, they are correct. There are now hundreds of tokens or protocols that have been built on Ethereum, while only a handful have been built on Bitcoin.

The individual known as a "Bitcoin Maximalist" is quite proud of the fact that securing the protocol has been the aim of the Bitcoin community rather than scale. The crypto hacks and scams that plague the community aren't actually related to Bitcoin, in fact, there has never been a hack of the Bitcoin network, though of course there have been hacks and scams related to exchanges where Bitcoin is traded. That these exchanges might operate in a questionable manner is not something Bitcoin should be blamed for, and in fact, when Bitcoin is viewed as a protocol, it should become clear that Bitcoin remains the purest of all cryptocurrencies.

To help emphasize this point, the crypto exchange / lending platform that was known as Celsius had a native token called CEL. This token was known as an "ERC 20" token, the Ethereum standard that allows for smart contract based token creation. The former CEO of Celsius, Alex Mashinsky is currently awaiting trial for his role in the exchange's collapse.

More well known than Mashinsky is Sam Bankman-Fried, former CEO of FTX, who in November of 2023, was found guilty on seven counts of fraud. His exchange also had a token that was often "pumped" to create a false sense of demand. That token, "FTT" was also an ERC 20 token. This of course is not to imply that everything being built on Ethereum is fraudulent, however, it is to say that Bitcoin and Ethereum are most certainly different, and in the quest to be faster and more scalable, Ethereum has left itself vulnerable to some of the worst actors in finance.

Prior to Celsius and FTX, there was another collapse that was a bit more contained to just the crypto world itself, that was the previously mentioned Terra Luna platform and its UST stablecoin. Headed by South Korean Do Kwon, Terra Luna's algorithmic backing meant that it employed a "burning" mechanism, by which there was an intricate interplay between the LUNA token and the platform's stablecoin UST. Like Mashinsky and SBF, Kwon is likely to soon be seeing jail time, and while the details aren't worth delving into here, a Do Kwon tweet from April 6th of 2022 is quite revealing. In that tweet, he mentioned having just bought $230M worth of Bitcoin. For the uninitiated, this purchase brought Bitcoin into the sad story of yet another crypto fail, but in reality, this was a last ditch effort on the part of Kwon to shore up his treasury. He was trying to create a sense of confidence in his ecosystem by bringing in more of the one asset that matters most: Bitcoin. Sadly, it was too late.

While Bitcoin at the protocol level can certainly be compared to SWIFT, it is XRP that is currently the platform that is most often seen as a potential competitor or replacement to SWIFT. The reason for

Bitcoin sometimes being left out of this discussion is really quite simple: XRP is a token that is issued by a company called Ripple. Being a company means there's a centralized leadership structure, and that leadership has been highly focused on building relationships with banks over the past several years. On many levels, they have been successful in building out a network of financial institutions, even while in the midst of their legal fight with the SEC, which they subsequently "won." I say "won" only because of the huge amount of time and money that was spent / lost defending themselves.

That Ripple and their XRP token should be mentioned here is important, as the XRP token serves as a sort of "bridge" currency for making cross border payments. PNC Financial Services here in the US, along with known brands such as American Express and Western Union, are all in some stage of exploring how XRP could better facilitate cross border payments.

When I first began investing in cryptocurrencies, I was warned against ever investing in tokens that you couldn't easily distinguish from the issuer, or the platform. In other words, Celsius should never have had to issue the CEL token if the platform worked the way they claimed. The same could be said for the FTT token used within FTX. I do not know whether XRP and Ripple will suffer the same fate as these others, but at present, it is difficult to see how Western Union needs XRP tokens when it appears they simply need access to the "Ripple Net" payment network.

That Ripple has major global partnerships that seem to be taking root can't be questioned, but to view these partnerships as a smooth road to market dominance may be a bit pre-mature. For example, in a June 2023 interview, MoneyGram CEO Alex Holmes, whose company was previously in a formal partnership with Ripple, made some rather cryptic comments regarding the Ripple / XRP solution. Principally, he asserted that the problem MoneyGram was trying to solve (high transaction fees stemming from foreign exchange challenges) was not made any better with XRP. In fact, he asserted that the problem was exacerbated with the introduction of the XRP token into the foreign exchange equation, not improved.

In addition to SWIFT and the traditional remittance protocols that XRP is competing against, there are also other crypto native protocols that are competing against XRP, with the most viable one being the XLM token that is part of the Stellar protocol. I am not aware of what makes Stellar a better solution than Ripple, but as of late 2023, MoneyGram now has a relationship with them.

As of late 2023, Bitcoin has not emerged as the protocol of choice for small, cross border remittance payments. Historically, the fees associated with these smaller transactions have simply been too high. Ripple or Stellar do potentially fill that void, but so too does the Lightning Network, a Bitcoin "side chain" that allows transactions to be "batched" very similarly to credit card transactions. This batching allows for Bitcoin to be used as a medium of exchange in ways that it has not been used previously. Should the Lightning Network gain traction, the use for something like XRP or XLM would certainly be minimized or even eliminated.

In mentioning XRP and XLM here, it make sense to briefly explore the idea of "tokenomics," which is the art/practice of examining a cryptocurrency through the lens of its token supply and issuance. This can be very important the farther away one gets from Bitcoin, because Venture Capital becomes a major part of the investment thesis. Bitcoin is sometimes said to have had a "virgin birth," because there is no company or known entity that gave birth to it. It exists without VC money, or private or public backing. The same simply can't be said for any other token or project.

Because of the manner in which tokens other than Bitcoin have been launched, there are now websites devoted to "token unlocks" which help investors see when vesting periods are about to expire, meaning there could be sell pressure. There are no token unlocks with Bitcoin, and in fact, the token issuance issue was the primary driver behind the SEC's lawsuit against Ripple and its XRP token, and is therefore the prime reason the SEC under Gary Gensler has been willing to admit that Bitcoin alone doesn't strictly come under his agency's purview as a security.

Token	Circulating Supply	Total Supply	Max Supply
XLM	28,163,962,839	50,001,787,069	50,001,787,069
XRP	54,005,597,115	99,988,151,135	100,000,000,000
BTC	19,570,881	21,000,000	21,000,000

Circulating Supply: comparable to stock shares currently available in the market at the present time.

Total Supply: comparable to outstanding stock shares, and can oftentimes be smaller than the Max Supply due to token "burning."

Max Supply: the theoretical maximum amount of coins permitted within the token's source code.

The chart above is intended to illustrate just two things:

1. XLM and XRP have almost proportionally identical coin supplies (XRP is roughly double that of XLM).
2. XLM and XRP have a lot more tokens out in the market than does BTC (Bitcoin).

In and of itself, the number of tokens does not scream "scam" or "scam free." What strikes me about XLM and XRP though, is the manner in which it is just so difficult to get a read on their tokenomics. The CoinGecko website used to provide the numbers in the chart below has a "tokenomics" section for many of the major coins on its site. When trying to get this information for both XLM and XRP, the following pops up:

"Tokenomics data for this coin is currently unavailable."

Both XLM and XRP fall within the top 25 tokens in terms of market capitalization. Within this top 25, nearly every other project's tokenomics can be clearly shown on the CoinGecko site, with the exception of BNB (Binance) a token and exchange currently involved in their own legal problems with US regulators. I have a hard time understanding the token issuance with either XLM or XRP. Coingecko apparently has the same problem.

The large volume of tokens that exist within these two protocols may turn out to be completely necessary to perfecting remittance payments on a global scale. I personally have a very small position with XRP right now on the off chance that a global cabal of traditional financiers has already made some sort of backroom deal with Ripple that its platform is the solution of choice for remittance payments in the future. That's hardly a rock solid investment thesis, and hardly something that is going to hold up to client scrutiny during your annual reviews. Quite simply: Bitcoin is not just different, it's much different.

3

BITCOIN AS A TECH STOCK

"The technology itself is not transformative. It's the application of technology that transforms."

~ Peter Drucker

One of Bitcoin's most ardent supporters over the past few years has been Microstrategy's Michael Saylor. While his name may not have the brand recognition of a Jobs or a Bezos, Saylor is no fool, and his company made the decision several years ago to begin using Bitcoin as its reserve asset. As Saylor is a long term believer in Bitcoin, he has seemingly not been caught up in the market swings of Bitcoin over the recent bear market, but rather, he has continued to educate others on its potential impact. One of his favorite ways of explaining Bitcoin is to visualize it as "stored energy."

This idea of Bitcoin as stored energy is directly tied to the "Proof Of Work" consensus mechanism mentioned previously. This concept is made more meaningful by the reality that Bitcoin mining, the process by which new Bitcoin are created, and also the process by which transactions fees are accumulated, is in fact a very energy intensive process. Bitcoin detractors are not wrong when they point out this fact, but in pointing out this fact, they also point out to why Bitcoin is potentially so important: because energy represents such a large percentage of a miners operational expenses, miners must go to where energy is the cheapest, and this means that Bitcoin has already had a major impact on distributing energy production more evenly around the globe.

Before delving into the veracity of what has just been stated, let us for just a brief moment ask the question: if there was a company that had the technology to evenly distribute the world's production of energy, would it be worth investing in such a company? To answer the question, one would perhaps need to gain some clarity via a few other inquiries. For example:

- Is energy production today unevenly distributed across geographic regions?
- Does this uneven distribution create energy bottlenecks?
- Does this uneven distribution contribute to global political tensions?

You have perhaps ascertained that I would answer all of the above questions in the affirmative, and as such, I would consider any technology capable of addressing these issues as potentially worthy of consideration for investment.

Having briefly mentioned the idea of Bitcoin mining, and having acknowledged that Bitcoin mining is in fact energy intensive, an example from the old school oil and gas industry is perhaps a good illustration of how the very concept of something being "energy intensive" is actually a relative concept.

Flared gas, which is natural gas that is burned off or "flared" as a byproduct of oil extraction or other industrial processes, can now be utilized to mine Bitcoin in a process being used throughout the US, especially in oil rich locations like Texas.

The first step in this process involves capturing the flared gas rather than letting it be released into the atmosphere. Once captured, the gas can be processed and converted into usable energy, thus powering generators or turbines that can in turn be used to power the Bitcoin mining equipment.

While Bitcoin mining used to be something that amateurs and smaller enthusiasts could participate in, the hardware requirements in use today have pushed out most smaller operations. The processors involved in mining are called "ASIC" or Application Specific Integrated Circuits and in addition to being somewhat costly, they have been created specifically for the purposes of mining. The capital outlay required means that "pools" represent more of Bitcoin's computational power today than when it was first created. It also means that large oil and gas producers are well suited to turn the formerly negative practice of flared gas into a positive re-purposing of wasted energy.

Obviously, the oil and gas industry is square in the cross hairs of those pushing for greener sources of energy, so simply eliminating the environmentally messy process of flaring is not likely to win many converts. There are other examples of truly green sources of energy that Bitcoin miners continue to migrate towards in the hopes of driving down their number one operating expense.

Perhaps the most recognized, and most interesting renewable energy provided to the Bitcoin network comes from the tiny nation of El Salvador. On September 7th of 2021, this Caribbean nation officially declared Bitcoin as legal tender. This action garnered severe rebukes from entities such as the International Monetary Fund along with the World Bank. Rather than backing down, El Salvador doubled down. Led by President Nayib Bukele, El Salvado now actively mines Bitcoin via energy supplied by some of the many dormant volcanoes located on the island.

"A fully renewable, untapped energy resource has been put to work strictly because of Bitcoin. Bitcoin is the greatest accelerant to renewable energy development in history."

~Bitcoin mining engineer Brandon Arvanaghi

As acknowledged previously, Bitcoin mining is energy intensive, but so is mining for gold. The last time I checked, the Amazon servers running all of the AWS platforms around the world weren't running on wind power or goodwill. What this means is that energy consumption isn't really about consumption per se, but rather about what is being derived from that consumption.

One of my personal favorite mental models of Bitcoin is as a global "truth machine." This description stems from the fact that the Bitcoin blockchain is known to be "immutable," meaning once a block has been validated, you can't go back and change it. This has enormous consequences across a variety of applications. For example, it is not difficult to see home titles, car titles, or other static type information being stored on the Bitcoin blockchain. Yes, there are other platforms that could provide this functionality, but again, none of them have shown the resiliency of Bitcoin up to this point.

This idea of a "truth machine" is not specific to the building of useful applications on top of the Bitcoin base layer. There are very meaningful ways in which a "truth machine" becomes incredibly meaningful in an era when transparency is demanded more and more. For example, many libertarians responded enthusiastically to former Congressman Ron Paul's cry to "audit the Fed." In a Bitcoin world, the need to audit as it is traditionally considered simply goes away. This happens for a few reasons, but one of them is mentioned here because it represents a concept that many never consider when exploring the payment options and the underlying payment "rails" upon which our modern payment infrastructure operates.

When a credit card gets swiped at a gas station, most users are given a choice: debit or credit. Upon making that selection, one enters either a PIN or ZIP, and immediately selects a fuel grade. Upon filling one's tank, an option to print out a receipt is provided, and the transaction is presumably completed. While the transaction is complete at a surface level, it most certainly isn't completed underneath the hood. You know this to be true because you have often looked at an online bank account and seen a charge as "pending." This is because credit card settlement does not occur at the point of sale, and in fact, may not occur for a few days. In a Bitcoin world, settlement is achieved roughly every 10 minutes, or every time a new block is validated.

The impact of this "peer to peer" payment system means that acceptance, settlement, and reconciliation all occur at roughly the same time. There is no need to "audit the Fed" in this system, as the audit happens in real time. There is no concept whereby one can move forward with a new block without having accurately and definitively settled the previous block.

It is because of the above reality that I personally do not believe that the US government is opposed to Bitcoin as a medium of exchange, or as "money." While we most certainly have been engaged in currency wars over the past several decades, I don't think there has ever been a push by US entities to try and eliminate local currencies of foreign nations. In many respects, most detractors have simply ridiculed Bitcoin as money, but it is hard to believe the US government has been any more concerned with Bitcoin than it would be with the Euro or the Yen. Rather, it is because of Bitcoin as an immutable "truth machine" that our policy makers likely ridicule it today.

The final application of Bitcoin as a tech stock comes from US Space Force Major Jason Lowry. Having received a Master's degree from MIT in Engineering and Management, Lowry recently published a book called *Softwar.* In that book, he takes Michael Saylor's concept of Bitcoin as "stored energy," one step further, and asserts that it is stored energy with a purpose, and that means, it is "power."

Prior to his joining Space Force, Lowry was with the Air Force, and attended its Command and Staff College, where he was introduced to the idea of the strategic "offset," a principal or concept by which a new technology could offset the historical strategic disadvantages one country may have previously had to endure in response to an adversary.

In an Open Letter to the United States Defense Innovation Board dated December 2nd 2023, Lowry asserted that Bitcoin is just such a potential offset. His thesis lies largely upon the idea that Bitcoin's Proof of Work consensus mechanism has ultimately created the world's most secure network, and in its present configuration, it is essentially open to all. Because of the open source nature of Bitcoin, Lowry has come to view Bitcoin as a way in which to envision "mutually assured preservation," this is because of the profound incentive structure that has given participants around the globe the confidence to continue using, securing, promoting, and developing the network.

In Lowry's letter, he sees Bitcoin has having the potential to play a significant role in our nation's cybersecurity efforts, but that will require us to see beyond Bitcoin's original use case as digital cash. He contends that while computer systems and the microchips that power them have gotten smaller with time, the Bitcoin network is potentially a "macrochip" that is so big, so ubiquitous, that the amount of effort and resources required to take it down become nearly impossible. Lowry therefore makes the logical leap that Bitcoin is something of a digital representation of what military deterrence has always been about: tilting the odds in such a way that even the most ardent aggressors must recognize that full scale attack is pointless.

It is worth noting that Lowry has detractors on all sides of this issue, from cybersecurity professionals who feel he doesn't properly understand the "access" problem of data security, to Bitcoin believers who are appalled that he would advocate for the weaponizing of the network. Regardless of one's opinions regarding Lowry's work, it seems to be obvious that he has realized something that few recognize: the very first block of the Bitcoin blockchain (the "Genesis" block) contained a message, and that message wasn't in reference to a financial transaction at all:

"Chancellor on brink of second bailout for banks"

Born out of the financial crisis known as the "GFC" or Great Financial Crisis, it has always been somewhat assumed that the message showed a disdain for central banks and cheap money. That is certainly plausible.

What this message did was also to "timestamp" the block in a rather creative way, by tying the first block to a definitive newspaper headline coming from The Times (London).

Part of Lowry's assertion is that secure communications are quite possible within a network like Bitcoin, and while he appears to be thinking in terms of military communications, it isn't hard to see diplomatic applications as well. It is here that many Bitcoin detractors begin to say things like, "Okay, I'm all onboard the idea of blockchain technology, but there's no way I'm going to put all my chips into an open source protocol like Bitcoin. I like the tech, but I'm going to build my own." What Lowry is positing, and is echoed by folks like Saylor, is that there is no way for another technology to come along and act like Bitcoin. Its "first mover advantage," is not just difficult to overcome, its not worth trying to overcome.

In this chapter, I have tried to make the case that Bitcoin can rightly be compared to a tech stock. I have made that assertion by exploring Bitcoin as a "company" with the technological capabilities to:

1. Evenly distribute energy production around the globe.
2. Serve as a global "truth machine" even without the need for coercion.
3. Serve as a cybersecurity protocol due to the distributed nature of the computational power behind the network, thus providing for a form of geopolitical influence and security far beyond the

traditional means.

If any of these three capabilities turn out to be true on a grand scale, Bitcoin would be an investment unlike anything currently traded on NASDAQ, or available to private investors. The point being made here in this chapter is further bolstered by the idea that the Securities and Exchange Commission, under the leadership of Gary Gensler, has only begrudgingly determined that Bitcoin does not fall under the jurisdiction of the SEC. I have written several articles in the past questioning Gensler's motives, but at some level, it seems plausible that Gensler sees Bitcoin as far more than money, or as something that should not simply fall under the Commodity Futures Trading Commission (CFTC).

As of late 2023, there is a "Futures ETF" for Bitcoin which is under the jurisdiction of the CFTC. There are applications from several of the world's largest asset managers currently being reviewed by the SEC that would create a "Spot ETF" for Bitcoin, and those ETFs would fall under the jurisdiction of the SEC. That there has been a digital asset turf war raging in Washington over the past several years is obvious, but in all fairness to these bureaucrats, Bitcoin is far more than money, so who should regulate it probably warrants some federal fistfights.

4

BITCOIN AS A HEDGE

*"The desire for gold is the most universal and deeply rooted
commercial instinct of the human race."*

~ Tacitus (Roman Historian)

One of the more challenging, or perhaps perplexing
aspects of studying and learning about the
cryptocurrency space is that there are plenty of respected
sources (people) who so firmly oppose the very concept.
One group of people who seem to be the most "anti-
crypto" are the supporters, backers, or holders of
precious metals, especially gold. Perhaps the most
visible of these crypto detractors is Peter Schiff, the well
known author, podcaster, and money manager. His
outspoken condemnations of Bitcoin make him a
favorite of the Bitcoin community when Bitcoin's price
goes up, and makes him something of a thorn when it
crashes.

Schiff is one of those people who often claim to
understand or see the value in blockchain technology,
but want nothing to do with the creation (Bitcoin) that
first made blockchain technology useful.

Anyone exploring Bitcoin needs to grasp the reality
that blockhain technology is not new. It has been
around for decades. What is new about Bitcoin, or
rather, what was revolutionary about Bitcoin, is the
"Proof Of Work" consensus mechanism that it employs.
It is because of this that Bitcoin is not simply another
payment system like PayPal or Visa. It is because of this
consensus mechanism that the need for a "trusted" third
party is eliminated. There is no "counter party risk"

involved with Bitcoin.

When someone like Schiff extols the virtue of blockchain technology while at the same time mocking Bitcoin, it's as though he's looking at a modern day automobile and getting excited about the fact that it comes equipped with a horn. "But you can alert your family when you arrive at home," he might be heard saying. Sure, the horn might be helpful at times, but it's certainly not what makes the car valuable.

What makes people like Schiff so confusing, is that his advocacy for things like sound money and fiscal responsibility are spot on. He knows our current economic conditions are littered with problems and sees Nixon's taking us off of the gold standard as a primary driver in our economic decline. He's not wrong.

Where Schiff seems to go astray is when he asserts that gold, and gold alone can serve as a form of hard money. That gold in physical form is not conducive to Internet based commerce seems to be a given, and so Bitcoin is today sometimes spoken of as "digital gold," so what drives Schiff to hate it so much, even mocking the very concept?

I would suggest that to Schiff, Bitcoin is an abstraction. At some level, I wonder if it is the comparisons to gold that have in some ways forced him to take an antagonistic stance. If Bitcoin's consensus mechanism was conducted via a group of computers known as "validators" instead of "miners," perhaps Schiff wouldn't be so antagonistic.

Beyond simple nomenclature though, Bitcoin's comparison to gold, which stems from the Proof of Work mechanism, means that the abstraction that Schiff mocks, is actually something of a bridge between the physical realm and the digital realm. In many respects, this is why Lowery's work is so important and worthy of discussion. With Bitcoin, we are talking about a true merger of the digital with the physical in a meaningful and important way: global finance. What is disappointing in Schiff's stance, is that if one is skeptical about such a merging, go challenge Meta CEO Mark Zuckerburg. Go debate the makers of virtual reality or augmented reality headsets, where the merging of the physical and digital is obvious, but at least at present, far less important.

This abstraction that Schiff and detractors like him struggle with also stems from the very true fact that gold is in fact aesthetically pleasing. A stack of silver coins is pretty easy on the eyes as well. I am aware that from beautiful cathedrals to beautiful jewelry, gold is almost universally acknowledged as physically appealing. It is also incredibly durable. These two properties are rightly lauded by Schiff, but the idea that something must have other, "real" world applications in order for it be a sound money is simply just not true. There are numerous historical examples that can be examined to substantiate my claim, but one of my favorites comes from the small Pacific island of Yap, where Rai stones were considered a form of money for many centuries. The use of Rai stones as a medium of exchange dates back to ancient times, and they continue to hold cultural and historical significance even today. The exact period of their use as money is challenging to pinpoint precisely due to the limited historical records from the region, but as a form of money, evidence suggests these stones were used well before the colonial period.

What makes the Rai stones such an interesting form of money, and pertinent to this study, is that these stones were not native to the island of Yap, but rather, they came from the limestone quarries located about 250 miles southwest of Yap on the island of Palau. The people of Yap would travel to Palau to quarry the large, circular discs of limestone and then transport them back to Yap for various purposes, including the creation of Rai stones. The transportation of these massive stones was often done using outrigger canoes, and the journey between Yap and Palau required careful navigation and significant effort.

If you have been following my line of thinking, you probably know what I'm about to write next: the use of Rai stones as money was not based on their usefulness in some other application, but simply because the presence of a Rai stone on the island of Yap was in fact, their version of "Proof of Work."

A couple of the attributes of this island monetary system are worth mentioning to hopefully drive home our point about money being an abstraction. First off, most of the stones were quite large, and due to this, they did not get moved around very often. This meant that a community recognized ledger is what allowed these large stones to be used as money. The big size also meant that this wasn't a very divisible form of money, so it typically was just used for large transactions, so in many respects, it served more as a "store of value" than it did as a day to day medium of exchange. Lastly, the concept of using the Rai stones as a form of money seems to have been a rather decentralized effort, as the community regulated it, seemingly without any coercion from above.

Can one primitive island nation's example really prove my point? That is up to you, but there are other examples of abstraction that also serve to bolster my contention. From diamond engagement rings to Super Bowl trophies, we know that these items are valuable because of what they represent. As I type these words in late December of 2023, the college football season has come to a close, at least the regular season with all of its rivalry games. For football fans, these rivalry games are a big part of the season, and one reason is the colorful trophies or awards given to the victors. While some of these trophies have material value, most are only valuable in what they represent. A short list of some of my favorites:

1. The Iron Skillet (yes, a literal iron skillet) which is awarded to the winner of the TCU vs SMU game.
2. Paul Bunyan's Axe which is awarded to the winner of the Minnesota vs Wisconsin game.
3. Old Brass Spittoon awarded to the winner of the Michigan State vs Indiana game.

None of these items, if not traditionally and emotionally tied to the institutions involved, would hold any sort of real value. For players, coaches, and fans alike, these trophies represent a very real "Proof of Work."

All of these examples have been offered here to simply try and give credence to the idea that Bitcoin just may become a true "digital gold." At current prices, gold represents a roughly $10T market, while Bitcoin represents a roughly $1T market. One Bitcoin is currently being traded at roughly $40,000. Should Bitcoin simply take 10% of gold's market share, it would be sitting at $80,000, and that would be assuming that everything else remained the same. As a financial planner, ask yourself: how many 20 to 30 year olds do you know of who are investing in gold? How many are investing in cryptocurrencies?

At some point over the past year, in the midst of our obviously chaotic market moves, I have probably heard the following adage a dozen times:

"You don't buy gold to get rich. You buy gold to stay rich."

This sentiment is something I completely agree with, and it points to what I hope is now abundantly clear: within our current economic system, gold is a great store of value, but the fact that it can be used to make nice jewelry isn't what gives it that property. What gives it that property is the fact that it takes work to get it out of the ground, and once out of the ground, it is basically indestructible.

This quality of gold, its durability, is something that Bitcoin most certainly can not claim. It is approximately 15 years old, but with each passing year, the network becomes more secure. With each passing year, the network comprises more users. In other words, with each passing year that it continues to exist, the more likely it becomes that it will exist in the future.

My assertion above has been articulated by Nicolas Taleb in his book *Antifragile*, in which he coins the term, the "Lindy Effect," named after the Lindy Theatre in New York City. The Lindy Theatre was a popular venue for Broadway shows, and the Lindy Effect was coined based on the idea that the future life expectancy of a non-perishable thing (such as a book, technology, or in this case, a Broadway musical) is proportional to its current age. Taleb used the Lindy Theatre as a heuristic to explain the principle. The longer a show had been running on Broadway, the more likely it was to continue running.

It is probably not hard to see how I view Bitcoin starting to adhere to this Lindy Effect, though as far as I know, Taleb is still not an advocate for Bitcoin adoption. As mentioned previously, the message contained within the first block of the Bitcoin blockchain referred to central bank bailouts. This has led many to speculate that Bitcoin's creator was something of a libertarian or anti-establishment activist. I have no special knowledge of Nakamoto's true identity or true intentions. What I do know, is that its "hard money" foundation, the idea that no more than 21 Bitcoin will ever be created, is something that must be considered by financial planners.

The idea of a fixed supply of something only has meaning if the thing that is being fixed is valuable. To someone like Schiff, who sees no value in Bitcoin, the fixed supply means nothing, so is he correct, does Bitcoin's fixed supply carry no meaning?

To address this question, it is useful to first compare Bitcoin to other cryptocurrencies to at least address "relative" value, in other words, to ascertain whether or not Bitcoin has value within the still somewhat limited realm of cryptocurrencies. While there are probably any number of ways to do this, I will keep it quite simple. Using data from CoinGecko:

Current Total Crypto Market Cap As of 12/12/2023	Current Total Number of Tokens (Projects) Listed As of 12/12/2023	Current Bitcoin Market Cap As of 12/12/2023
$1.63T	11,394	$809,053,996,077

Amongst crypto traders, the number I'm working towards is called "Bitcoin Dominance." This number is something paid attention to because it serves as a barometer that helps identify when it might be safe to jump into more dubious "alt coins."

Based on the figures above, Bitcoin accounts for roughly 53% of the entire crypto market. Looked at another way, the Bitcoin protocol, which represents just .00877655% of all the current crypto protocols in existence, accounts for more than 50% of the market value. I do not know what the exact terms is for such market dominance but for now, I will simply say that Bitcoin clearly has "relative market strength."

As an investor, what Bitcoin's relative market strength means on a practical level is that there is no crypto market without Bitcoin. It is what drives the entire market. At present, there are approximately 900 centralized crypto exchanges in the world. None of them exist without Bitcoin. The Chinese have banned Bitcoin and Bitcoin mining so many times most observers have stopped paying attention. It simply refuses to die.

Many investors in emerging technologies are often quick to point out that Facebook (Meta) was not the first of the social networks, but rather, came on the heals of MySpace. This is true. There are certainly other examples or instances in which being a comfortable second entry into the marketplace proved providential and eventually profitable. I would still contend that for every Facebook overtaking MySpace, there is a USFL struggling for relevance against the NFL.

As it pertains strictly to crypto, the Bitcoin moat is now so substantial, that even its competitors do not want to see it lose market share. In other words, of the thousands of cryptocurrencies vying for market share today, perhaps only a handful of them actually want to even be compared to Bitcoin. These include a few other

Proof of Work currencies like Litecoin and Bitcoin Cash. Both of these currencies are "forks" of the original Bitcoin protocol and because of their larger block sizes, they are in fact better at present for smaller transactions. Unfortunately for them, the market doesn't care. Bitcoin Cash has a market share roughly 200 times smaller than Bitcoin. Litecoin is only marginally larger.

As it pertains to the crypto market at large, Bitcoin isn't just a major player, it is the player. Yes, there will always be new protocols like Ethereum that emerge and do in fact have viable use cases, but they won't actually be competing with Bitcoin. Those in the space, from developers to VC firms, do not even think in terms of becoming "the next Bitcoin." They do think in terms of being the next Ethereum, which is why many feel like SOL (Solana) will be the token of choice in the next bull run, with other contenders like AVAX (Avalanche) and ADA (Cardano) hot on their heels.

As this chapter is dedicated to your viewing Bitcoin as a potential hedge, what this means is that you might include it in your asset allocation based simply on the idea that Web3, the metaverse, and AI will all require methods to move value in ways that traditional finance simply does not facilitate. Bitcoin does.

I am not a "Bitcoin Maximalist," as I do recognize that there are other cryptos that have interesting and meaningful use cases. For example, several platforms are using blockchain technology to allow musicians to "own" their creations, promote their work, grow their fanbases, and subsequently gain a much greater share in the profits. I'm perfectly fine living in a world where record labels can't exploit artists. There are at least 13 tokens purely devoted to that aim. I haven't a clue as to which one might emerge as the clear winner, and neither do you. Fortunately, you need not concern yourself with the outcome of the "Great Blockchain Based Musicians Debate." Bitcoin will get you a responsible amount of exposure with far less risk.

5
BITCOIN AS HOPE

"When I had money everyone called me brother."

~ Polish proverb

In the United States, it is sometimes difficult to propose Bitcoin or crypto as a lifeboat for when financial conditions go south, because we quite frankly have not had much experience with such an event. Whether we can attribute that to luck, the rule of law, or two really big oceans separating us from potential adversaries, most Americans do not make financial decisions based on any sort of real probabilities that our banking system could collapse or that political conditions could deteriorate to the point of needing to find refuge overseas.

While Americans might not currently be planning for such circumstances, entire regions of the world are quite familiar with these sorts of events. From runaway inflation in Argentina to "bail ins" in Cyprus, ordinary citizens have suffered greatly in the wake of financial meltdowns.

While not a crypto company per se, Chainalysis is one of the more interesting entities within the crypto space. Its tools have become well known for their ability to help law enforcement track down criminal activity on the various blockchain protocols. To many hardcore libertarians in the space, Chainalysis and its people are barely one step above central bankers in terms of moral depravity. I personally am cognizant of the fact that if bad actors are going to do bad things, then tools are going to be created to minimize the damage. I support that. At the same time, some of the tactics employed by

Chainalysis makes me more than a bit nervous.

With that "disclaimer" out of the way, I have turned to an annual report published by Chainalyis regarding crypto adoption across the globe. Few entities are capable of providing such an accurate study, and for this type of insight, I applaud them.

In their most recent study for 2023, they certainly pointed out that crypto adoption is down from the previous highs that coincided with Bitcoin's rise to just over $69,000. While that was not news, what stood out was the manner in which crypto adoption has accelerated by 40% in what the World Bank designates as "Lower Middle Income" countries. Examples of countries that fall into this category include India, Nigeria, and Ukraine. The narrative that comes with such findings is somewhat easy to craft: adoption is strongest in those countries where both economic opportunity and economic struggles exist side by side.

What the study also shows is that slowing retail adoption in developed nations has in many ways been offset by institutional adoption. Again, the populations of High Income (HI) countries might not currently be flocking to crypto, but the financial institutions in those HI countries most certainly are. As the reports states:

"This could be extremely promising for crypto's future prospects. LMI countries are often countries on the rise, with dynamic, growing industries and populations. Many of them have undergone significant economic development in the last few decades to rise from the low income group. And perhaps most importantly of all, ***40% of the world's population live in LMI countries — more than any other income category.*** *If LMI countries are the future, then the data indicates that crypto is going to be a big part of that future. That, combined with the fact*

that institutional adoption, primarily driven by organizations in high-income countries continues to gain steam even during the ongoing crypto winter, paints a promising picture of the future. We could see a combination of bottom up and top down cryptocurrency adoption in the near future if these trends hold, as digital assets fulfill the unique needs of individuals in both segments."

The idea of Bitcoin as a tool, instrument, or asset in troubled times is something that has been promulgated by enthusiasts almost from the very beginning. If one holds their Bitcoin keys on a hardware wallet, it is nearly like having a Swiss bank account on a thumb drive. Clearly, it's much easier to cross a border with a thumb drive than with a pull cart full of gold. Again, this attribute has been made by many, and as this book is geared more towards financial planning and investment theory, I won't attempt to bolster that line of thinking.

Rather, what I do think is worth building upon is the idea that Bitcoin might eventually serve as a psychological lifeboat for long term investors. Before going further, let me make a point that perhaps should have been made earlier:

There is no long term future in which Bitcoin remains in the vicinity of $42,000 (where it is currently trading as I write this).

In the long term, which I would define as roughly two Bitcoin "halving cycles" or roughly 8 years, Bitcoin is either moving towards zero, or it is moving towards $500,000. I say this with a great deal of confidence, acutely aware of the fact that Bitcoin's adoption rate either accelerates or decelerates, and in either case, it will be something of a fly wheel effect. There will be no middle ground.

If I am correct, this means that investing in Bitcoin today has something like a 12x upside. Again, I'm not discounting the fact that it might go to zero, but a 12x upside potential is what can accurately be labeled as an "asymmetric" bet.

In a recent interview with an investor whose name I can not remember, he mentioned that he typically, but not always, avoids trading with leverage. One of the ways in which he somewhat simulates leverage is to buy stocks in gold mining companies when he feels gold is entering a long term bull market. In other words, the price action he's going to get out of the miners is far more than he's going to get out of the spot price of gold. If he's wrong, he doesn't have to face liquidation issues.

In many respects, Bitcoin is lot like this leveraged gold miner strategy. Yes, for some, Bitcoin still feels risky, but as I've tried to articulate, at least within the crypto industry itself, Bitcoin is on very solid ground. Because of where we now are in Bitcoin's adoption cycle, I would contend that it is psychologically sound bet to make.

As this book is intended for those with some form of financial responsibility, it is perhaps not proper to use the word "bet," so I'll offer up the term "asymmetric opportunity" instead. Regardless of what you might prefer, I think one of the healthiest outlooks which we as individuals can have centers around the idea of "hope."

So aside from the strategic attributes of a Bitcoin position, I believe investing in Bitcoin today, in the midst of very real economic and geopolitical tensions, is psychologically sound. But the volatility! Yes, there is volatility with Bitcoin, but those glorious green candles on the charts when it is pumping are pure magic. I would assert that in stable times, having a roller coaster of an asset like Bitcoin would not equate to mental wellness for most. In our current era though, Bitcoin's potential, its possibilities: possessing even just a little of that hope is no doubt a good thing.

This idea of Bitcoin being psychologically sound hit me recently while on a treadmill at my local gym. There are televisions everywhere, and they're all typically turned to Fox News or ESPN. The volume is usually muted, so unless you've got headphones on, one is typically just seeing headlines scrolling along the bottom. What is striking to me about the scrolling headlines is how "hopeful" they often are for the demographic that is being catered to. In the case of Fox News, the scrolling words describe Biden's sinking polling numbers, Hunter Biden's inevitable jail time, or the Vice President's latest international speaking engagement running off the rails.

The scrolling headlines make the person inclined to watch Fox News very hopeful for the future failings of the left. Of course, the CNN's of the world do the very same thing to their audience, pumping them full of hopium that has them convinced that Donald Trump will soon be banished to the island of Elba. During Trump's impeachment, it was quite clear that most left leaning Americans were clearly of the belief that being impeached was the equivalent of Trump going to jail. They were quite disappointed when that hope was dashed.

Fox, CNN, MSNBC, and all the others know a few things about marketing. They know a great deal about crafting a narrative, and to a great degree, I think the overall strategy can be summarized as:

Hate (your opponent) + Hope (your opponent

suffers) = I Am a Good Person

This simultaneous mixing of hate and hope is something that many of us know is toxic. It has driven a wedge through our country, and yet, we seem almost powerless to stop it, or to at least walk away from it. Assuming for a moment that I am correct and that hate and hope are playing an outsized role in today's America, what if one could have hope without the hate?

One of the most powerful voices in the crypto space today comes from a guy named Preston Pych. He has hosted a finance podcast for about 9 years and has slowly morphed into a very respected Bitcoin advocate. One of the reasons he resonates with me is because he often speaks of how Bitcoin will soon be the preferred money of producers, while fiat currencies will remain the preferred money of the consumers (the takers).

There are a few implications for this opinion often expressed by Pych, but one that I keep coming back to is that consumptive behavior is typically very "me" and "now" centric. On the other hand, having a production mindset is very "others" centric, with a future facing orientation. This idea is really where the ESG / Sustainability Crowd truly gets exposed: it is consumptive behavior that is unsustainable or potentially dangerous for the environment and that stems from the monetary mindset of our leaders that quite obviously operates under a "no limits" mindset, a mindset that simply can't exist under a Bitcoin standard.

6
WHERE IS BITCOIN?

"I think the internet is going to be one of the major forces for reducing the role of government. The one thing that's missing but that will soon be developed, is a reliable e-cash."

~Nobel Prize Winning Economist Milton Friedman

In most studies or discussions of money, it is almost conventional wisdom to acknowledge that money goes through stages on its journey to actually becoming money in the way that we normally think of it. The better the form of money, the more steps will be made in the journey. The steps involved typically goes something like this:

1. This new form of money first serves as nothing more than a collectable (seashells, glass beads, NFTs).
2. As the collectible becomes more mainstream, these collectibles become a medium of exchange, if only within a few groups, markets, or economies.
3. Eventually enough people feel compelled or incentivized to hold onto the currency that it begins to be viewed as a store of value.
4. Finally, the money becomes universally used or so widely accepted, that it becomes a unit of account.

At present, Bitcoin is somewhere between steps 2 and 3. It must be acknowledged that these steps don't always move in a perfect linear manner, but one thing that Saifedean Ammous has clearly articulated, is that "being a medium of exchange is the quintessential function that defines money – in other words, it is a good purchased not to be consumed (a consumption good), nor to be employed in the production of other goods (an investment or capital good), but primarily for the sake of being exchanged for other goods"[3]

It is because of my agreeing so much with Ammous that I make the contention that serves as the title of this book: Bitcoin is not just money, because ultimately, it is more than simply a medium of exchange. In fact, it is perhaps more accurately described as a "medium of expression."

I wish so badly to be able to claim this "medium of expression" as my own, but it comes from Seb Bunney, something of self-taught economist and educator whose phrasing hit me like a ton of bricks when I first heard it. The day I heard this phrase, I brought it up to my family at dinner. Only my younger three boys were at the table with my wife and I. We were wrapping up dinner when my kids probably saw that look in my eyes, the look that so often says, "okay kids, try to pretend you're interested, but we're going to have a short economics lesson."

Perhaps I was a bit too eager, perhaps I was a bit too expressive. Whatever the case was, my kids were less than impressed, not because the "medium of expression" didn't strike them as true, but because it struck them as so obvious.

While hardly an exact quote, one of my boys said something like, "well yeah…if you're a kid spending all your money on video games, you're telling all the world you're a gamer and you like jumping online and playing

---

[3]Ammous, Saifedean. *The Bitcoin Standard.* Hoboken, NJ: John Wiley & Sons, 2018.

with friends. If you're buying nothing but Legos, you're telling the world you like to hang out by yourself."

Typically speaking, money as a means of expression has been confined to the "what" of the transaction. As my kids intuitively knew, what you buy tells people about you. What you use to facilitate the transaction has really never before expressed a great deal. To be sure, if you stroll into a car dealership today and pull out 30 ounces of gold to purchase a new vehicle, you are certainly saying something. On the aggregate though, these types of transactions are nearly non-existent.

With the emergence of Bitcoin though, the idea of money as a medium of expression takes on much more meaning, because the method being used now says something about you, not just what was being purchased by the exchange. Perhaps you balk at my assertion, but right now, should you have a used set of golf clubs for sale online, and I message you asking if you were set up and capable of accepting Bitcoin, I am telling you things about me. I would contend that I'm expressing to you that:

1. I'm at least technically proficient enough to know how to send Bitcoin from wallet to wallet.
2. I have at least a marginal interest in seeing Bitcoin adoption increase.
3. I know that turning my Bitcoin into cash is definitely a taxable event in the US, so I'm at least economically astute enough to know it is probably better for all involved if we can transact without me having to convert Bitcoin into something you do accept.

While these three things might be considered positive, it

is certainly possible that on the other hand, you as the owner of the clubs might be viewing things somewhat differently:

1. This guy is an idiot, why is he selling his Bitcoin?
2. Golfers aren't usually anarchists, why is he into Bitcoin?
3. Doesn't this guy just use Venmo like everyone else?

Regardless of the validity of the above scenario, with the emergence of Bitcoin, the method with which we choose to conduct transactions now means something, not just the "thing" we receive as a result of the transaction. This phenomenon, which in some ways is like voting, is not entirely new though, as we know that there have been times in history when coins, currencies, and other payment methods have battled for supremacy. We simply haven't had such a battle for about a century, and even then, the battle was fought by regulators and policy makers, certainly not by individuals.

What is completely new about Bitcoin as a medium of expression in today's era, is that in many respects, it is a vote for sound money. It is a vote for transparency. It is a vote for equal financial footing for the masses. In other words, never before has a currency's use said so much within one's nation's borders as Bitcoin does. Again, Americans may not be quite aware of this just yet, but the residents of El Salvador most certainly are, as are the Argentinians. Canadian truck drivers are pretty aware of it as well.

Of all the narratives that are sometimes attributed to Bitcoin, it is certainly the "anti-inflationary" one this is the most easily explained to the retail investor. At the institutional or professional level, this fixed supply nature of Bitcoin is often glossed over, as though perhaps it is such a simple concept, and so readily understood, that it must not really be an attribute that sophisticated investors need understand.

I believe that part of the reason for the dismissive attitude surrounding the fixed supply attribute of Bitcoin is that for many in the financial sector, another dogma that has readily been accepted, is that inflation is necessary for a growing economy. This supposed need for some level of inflation apparently comes from the erroneous belief that the velocity of money will so profoundly decrease in a deflationary environment, that our economy will come to a standstill.

This belief is widely held in both academia and Washington, yet even just a simple analysis tells us that it just isn't true. There is not an economist alive who would contest the idea that technology is by its very nature deflationary. A John Deere tractor allows for acres of land to be farmed by a single worker. An Internet connection and some software allows Turbo Tax to do tax filings at scale, charging far less than the standard CPA firm. There should be no debate that technology is deflationary, and we are currently living in the most technologically advanced period in human history. This reality has been expressed by Canadian entrepreneur and author Jeff Booth. He goes so far as to claim that "deflation is the key to an abundant future."[4]

Booth's assertion is worth examining for a host of different reasons, but he is interesting to me not so much for what he says or thinks, but the manner in

---

[4] Booth, Jeff. The Price of Tomorrow. Stanley Press, 2020.

which he becomes difficult to classify. He is a former CEO and founder. He's a technologist with a philosophy that strives to make the economic pie bigger for everyone, rather than ensuring he simply gets a bigger share. In his book, he speaks a good bit about the narratives and stories humans latch onto in order to make sense of the world. One narrative he mentions specifically is the "hero" narrative, and he quotes a 1997 Apple marketing campaign to help make the point:

> *Here's to the crazy ones. The misfits. The rebels. The troublemakers. The round pegs in the square holes. The ones who see things differently. They're not fond of rules. And they have no respect for the status quo. You can quote them, disagree with them, glorify or vilify them. About the only thing you can't do is ignore them. Because they change things…They push the human race forward…While some may see them as the crazy ones, we see genius. Because the people who are crazy enough to think they can change the world are the ones who do.*

While Booth quotes the above campaign as a means of showing the power of narrative and emotion, I include it to help shed light on the reality that Bitcoin is indeed hard to evaluate, it is hard to put into a box, because *where* one puts it depends on *where* one sees it fitting in to their overall narrative that has been crafted over time.

As mentioned previously, dogmas per se don't offend me. When I enter a busy traffic roundabout, I'm not bemoaning rules. When I turn on a computer and it works, I'm not upset that the software engineers have employed a strict sense of discipline in their design principles. It hopefully becomes apparent that I'm not advocating for a Bitcoin standard out of a sense of anarchy, but rather, from a sense of fairness.

Within the Bitcoin community, there is the general feeling that everything, or at least nearly everything we encounter in our world today is "downstream of money." While the absolute truth of the phrase is debatable, the assertion comes in large part from what is known as the "Cantillon Effect," named after the 18th century economist Richard Cantillon.

The assertion made here refers to the uneven impact that changes in the money supply have on prices and economic activity. More specifically: when new money is injected into an economy, it doesn't spread uniformly. The individuals or entities that receive the new money first can benefit significantly, as they can spend it before prices have adjusted to the increased money supply. On the other hand, those who receive the new money later or not at all may experience rising prices without the benefit of increased income.

In essence, the Cantillon Effect highlights the fact that the distribution of money in an economy matters. Changes in the money supply don't affect all individuals and sectors equally, and the timing and channels through which money enters the economy can have significant implications for wealth distribution and economic dynamics.

In case you are wondering, there was no mention of the Cantillon Effect in my Economics upbringing at the Naval Academy. I only heard of it upon learning about Bitcoin, but whether you believe in Bitcoin or not, you intuitively know that Cantillon was correct: if money supplies are going to expand and contract, whoever knows about those events ahead of time will benefit disproportionately. Bitcoin has a known supply, upon reaching 21M, there is no more "Quantitative Easing" that can create more. That is a system that negates the power of the Cantillon Effect, that is a system that is inherently fair, where insider knowledge isn't necessary in order to financially thrive.

The Bitcoin advocates I know of aren't in fact "troublemakers," but they do see major trouble brewing with unsustainable debt levels being the most obvious point of failure for our economic system. Ray Dallio has written and spoken of debt cycles for years, and he, along with a host of other financial leaders all seem to be pointing to some sort of reckoning that will be nearly impossible to avoid. Just where Bitcoin falls into that reckoning seems like a worthy academic exercise, and so the preceding chapters have been my attempt to show that Bitcoin is far more than a monetary instrument (digital or otherwise). I have attempted to provide a few different frameworks for trying to look at it, or to give it a fair valuation. Thus far:

1. Bitcoin as a protocol, something upon which other applications can be built.
2. Bitcoin as a tech stock.
3. Bitcoin as a hedge.
4. Bitcoin as hope.

To be fair, some of these frameworks have a bit of overlap with each other (hedge and hope aren't widely different), but for the most part, asking "what is it" in regards to Bitcoin is quite healthy. I started off seeing it as nothing more than digital money with an anti-inflationary narrative. After nearly 6 years in the space, I've barely scratched the surface with regards to what it is, what all it could be used for, and how it might emerge within a globally conflicted economic system.

While first seeking to describe what Bitcoin is, or at

least what it could be, it now seems appropriate to address the question, "where is Bitcoin?" I will address this along three lines:

1. Where it is in terms of adoption.
2. Where it is in terms of regulation.
3. Where it is in terms of hash rate (computational power)

Adoption

As it pertains to adoption, Bitcoin does not lend itself to traditional tracking methods. For example, trying to measure cell phone adoption in the early 2000's was rather straightforward: one cell phone owner looked pretty much like every other cell phone owner (at least from the vantage point of the carrier doing the billing). In crypto, the same can't be said. For example, if you set up a Coinbase account for your Aunt Alice and she never logs in except during bull markets when you're at her house for Thanksgiving, should she be included as an adopter?

From miners, to small node operators, to institutional investors, it is nearly impossible to accurately assess crypto adoption in general and Bitcoin adoption specifically. Despite this difficulty, there are various methods by which researchers have come up with the magic number of 22% of US households currently holding some portion of a Bitcoin. Because of Bitcoin's youth, it is still possible to visibly represent this rate of adoption in a small table:

Year	Percentage of US Households Owning Some Quantity of Bitcoin
2009	0%
2010	0.5%
2011	1.5%
2012	3%
2013	4%
2014	5%
2015	6%
2016	7%
2017	8%
2018	9%
2019	10%
2020	13%
2021	15%
2022	17%
2023	22%

The simplicity of this table is on purpose. In terms of a protocol, these adoption rates are not mind blowing, but they do mimic something like the addition of the SSL to HTTP, which gave us HTTPS and made online payments and financial applications possible. Netscape first introduced that in 1995, with Yahoo being one of the last to make it "standard" by 2012. As of 2023, Google claims that 95% of its sites and servers are "HTTPS" by default.[5] Without assuming or extrapolating too much, that's a 28 year journey to 95% adoption.

What about pure technology plays like cell phones?

---

[5] https://transparencyreport.google.com/https/overview

As of 2023, Pew Research estimates that 97% of Americans have a cell phone of some kind. That seems reasonable, but what surprises many, is that Motorolla introduced the first commercially available cell phone in 1973, meaning that is has taken 50 years to reach near universal adoption in the US. As a technology, Bitcoin is well ahead of that pace.

In terms of Bitcoin's adoption, it would appear it is being adopted about the way protocols have been adopted in the past, though certainly a bit faster than some. One of the major benefits of my making the claim that Bitcoin is not just money, is that you will hopefully give me a pass for not doing a historical analysis of monetary adoption rates. Perhaps such an analysis is possible, but would it prove anything? The manner in which the Phoenicians started using gold, or the speed at which cigarettes first began to be used as money in US prisons would reveal what about Bitcoin's monetary adoption? I would contend that it would reveal very little, and help you, even less.

While adoption rate methodologies are far from uniform across different technologies, Bitcoin does seem to be adhering to the same sort "S Curve" that major technological innovations usually end up adhering to. There is another means of examining adoption that also bears mentioning here, and that is the adoption amongst developers and software engineers. This is not a perfect "adoption" methodology, as it implies staying power a bit more than adoption, it does help give investors and observers a manner of identifying what protocols are being built upon. As derived by GitHub developer commit data aggregated by CryptoMiso,[6] the following

---

[6] https://www.cryptomiso.com/

table tells an interesting story.

Rank	Past 12 Months	Past 9 Months	Past 6 Months	Past 3 Months
1	ICP	ICP	ICP	ICP
2	SUSHI	SUSHI	SUSHI	SUSHI
3	MINA	MINA	MINA	SOL
4	SOL	SOL	SOL	NEAR
5	CAKE	CAKE	LINK	LINK
6	LINK	LINK	CAKE	CAKE
7	MASK	MASK	MASK	RBC
8	GRS	GRS	BTCB	NXM
9	BTCB	BTCB	GRC	ATOM
10	BTC	BTC	BTC	STORJ

Over the past 12 months, with the market being very muted amidst a variety of headwinds, Bitcoin (BTC) was in the top ten in terms of developer "activity." Actually, BTCB represents Bitcoin related developer activity but on the Binance smart chain, so technically, it could be thought of as BTC related building. Regardless, the story remains: when economic conditions seemingly improve, developer activity does migrate to other chains, as recent developer activity has spread to lesser known protocols. Bitcoin is not shown on the table for the past 3 months, as it fell to number 18.

As an investor seeking to gain a bit more understanding of Bitcoin, it is worth knowing that in some circles, it is considered a "Boomer Coin," an almost boring component of the crypto ecosystem. It uses C++ as opposed to something like "Rust" or "Go." Creativity is not the hallmark of C++ and younger developers aren't exactly flocking to it should they be pursing a career in this field. What the numbers imply though, is that developer activity on the Bitcoin platform remains very strong, albeit a bit weaker when market conditions seemingly improve (interest rate hikes at least being paused).

Regulation

Up until this point, every word I have typed has been with a sense of excitement, enthusiasm, or anticipation. This section, dedicated to regulation, is my version of a root canal: painful but necessary. Were I not to devote a few words to this subject, I would be doing you a great disservice, and would be potentially setting you up for some real issues.

The following is as succinct as I can be without being truly negligent:

In the early years following the invention of Bitcoin, roughly 2009 to 2012, there was nearly no regulatory oversight, as cryptocurrencies were for the most part, simply not recognized by governments. Regulatory agencies seemed to have begun paying attention by around 2013 as Bitcoin had by this time gained a bit of popularity, and other cryptocurrencies were being created. By 2015, there were some countries issuing consumer warnings, but formal regulations were very limited.

In October of 2013, and February of 2014, two major events occurred that would have long term implications for the crypto space. First, the anonymous "dark web" marketplace known as Silk Road was penetrated by federal agents and shut down. The administrator and creator of the site, Ross Ulbricht, was charged with money laundering, computer hacking, and narcotics trafficking. He is currently serving a life sentence without the possibility of parole. The use of cryptocurrency, primarily Bitcoin, was the preferred method of exchange on his site.

In early 2014, Mt. Gox was the world's largest crypto exchange. If you wanted Bitcoin, this was basically where you started. Located in Tokyo, its CEO was Frenchman Mark Karpeles.

The demise of Mt. Gox started when approximately 850,000 Bitcoin could not be accounted for and trading had to be halted. By April, the company had declared bankruptcy, with Karpeles being arrested for embezzlement and data manipulation. In 2019, Karpeles was found guilty of falsifying financial records, but he was acquitted of embezzlement charges. He ended up serving no jail time, as he seemed to be more negligent than nefarious.

There has been an ongoing, and moderately successful effort in trying to recover the missing Bitcoin and there is currently a court appointed trustee in charge of the process by which Mt. Gox customers are at least getting some of their money back. Ironically, because these were actual Bitcoin, and not just dollars or yen, those customers who have gotten their Bitcoin back have made handsome profits. Silk Road and Mt. Gox, more specially, their demise, served as seminal events in that regulators across the globe were now paying attention to crypto and crypto based crime.

By 2016, several countries, not surprisingly, including Japan, started to introduce regulatory frameworks for cryptocurrencies. Within the US, the Financial Crimes Enforcement Network (FinCEN) began providing guidelines regarding the application of money transmission laws to virtual currencies.

By 2017, there was a boom in what the industry knows as an "ICO" or Initial Coin Offering. Similar to an IPO, these coin offerings led to a huge surge in fundraising and unfortunately also a huge surge in scams. Both the fundraising and the scams prompted regulators across the globe to issue warnings and guidelines regarding the legal status of ICOs. Ripple Labs never issued its XRP token via an ICO, which is interesting in that the SEC clearly sees these ICOs as illegal, but ended up suing XRP anyway. XLM (Stellar) did conduct an ICO in 2014.

By 2018, the ICO craze had been dampened and "crypto winter" set in. Regulators continued to explore ways to regulate the industry, focusing on investor protection and preventing fraud. In 2019, Facebook's announcement of the Libra (now Diem) project brought heightened regulatory scrutiny. Concerns about consumer protection, privacy, and potential systemic risks prompted discussions among global regulators, and the project was eventually scuttled. In short, Facebook was trying to create a currency within its application and regulators said no.

The central bank low interest rate policies and Quantitative Easing (QE) that characterized the entire COVID-19 era led to an increased interest in digital assets as an alternative investment. Institutional adoption of cryptocurrencies also grew, being largely fueled by executives like Michael Saylor and Jack Dorsey who publicly advocated for Bitcoin adoption. During this time, the market also saw the rise of Non-Fungible Tokens (NFTs), and because these were largely cryptographic cartoon pictures trading for thousands of dollars, the regulators became even more confused. Digital money is obviously one thing, but digital monkeys is another thing all together. At the end of 2020, the SEC issued its lawsuit of Ripple Labs.

On March 9th of 2022, President Biden signed "Executive Order on Ensuring Responsible Development of Digital Assets." This order had been anticipated for several weeks, and while it was highly anticipated within the crypto community, the order itself was short on specifics, long on bureaucratic jargon, and therefore subject to speculation by anyone who bothered reading it.

In this admittedly abbreviated overview of events, there was a standard theme within the industry: innovation of all types (creative, criminal, pointless, and profound) and confused regulators struggling to find the right balance. Developed nations like the US have certainly had different regulatory approaches than developing nations. What US regulators have sometimes seen as a threat, smaller nations have clearly seen as an opportunity. This should not come as a surprise. What has been surprising though, is the shotgun manner in which many US regulators, some politicians, and most traditional finance executives have sought to combat the potential threat.

The best example of this poor response comes from the SEC under Gary Gensler. Rather than helping provide helpful guidelines, his agency has opted for the lawsuit, going so far as to claim that everything besides Bitcoin is a security, and if not registered with the SEC, one is operating illegally. This stance is laughable on its face. The primary legal precedence for what constitutes a security comes from the "Howey Test" stemming from a 1940's era case that established the criteria by which something should be labeled a security. There are four main elements to this litmus test, and all must be present for a transaction to be classified as an investment contract:

1. Investment of money
2. Common enterprise (the investor's money must be pooled with that of others, and the returns must be derived from the efforts of a third party or a promoter. In other words, the investors are relying on the managerial or entrepreneurial efforts of others)
3. Expectation of profits
4. Efforts of others

The most egregious statements that Gensler has made regarding cryptocurrencies and securities law is when he has asserted that some stablecoins are also securities.[7] As the entire point of a stablecoin is to remain pegged to the underlying currency, it is quite clear that no profit is being pursued by holding the stablecoin. There is no "expectation of profits" when it comes to stablecoins, regardless of how the issuer of the stablecoin attempts to keep the peg.

Perhaps less egregious than stablecoins, Gensler has also hinted that NFTs just might fall under securities laws.[8] I only say "less egregious" because it is possible that someone might be purchasing an NFT for the purposes of profit, unlike a stablecoin which is clearly being purchased for its "stability." Going this route means that the SEC under Gary Gensler is potentially gunning for issuers of baseball cards, Cabbage Patch

---

[7] https://finance.yahoo.com/news/sec-chair-hints-stablecoins-securities-161700741.html

[8] https://fortune.com/crypto/2023/08/28/sec-nfts-securities-impact-theory-dapper-yuga-crypto-gensler/

Dolls, and any other collectible that he has a problem with. Guidance from Gensler was assumed by crypto advocates when he took over as chairman because he'd been at MIT where he taught courses devoted to blockchain technology. Rather than guidance, the space is now connected to graft, as there is more than mere speculation that Ginsler had improper connections to Sam Bankman Fried and the fraudulent FTX.

Admittedly, reading the preceding events is probably even less fun than me writing them. As someone in charge of other people's money, you would be well within your rights to take a "steer clear" approach. On the regulatory front, it's not all bad news though, and in fact, there are reasons to be optimistic.

First off, the SEC was forced to settle with Ripple Labs in late 2023. I have no foundational attachments to Ripple or its executives, but this seemed like heavy handed overreach on the part of the SEC from the very beginning. As an investor, this is good news because it means the SEC can't just fire off crypto lawsuits and expect rubber stamp victories.

Secondly, there are now numerous lawmakers in Congress who are openly supportive of sensible crypto adoption. From Democrat Ritchie Torres in the House, to Republican Cynthia Lummis in the Senate, there is a growing number of politicians who actually understand digital assets. To be fair, there is not total agreement amongst this growing list of pro-crypto lawmakers, but almost across the board, they see Bitcoin as a financial force for good.

Thirdly, on December 13th of 2023, the Financial Accounting Standards Board (FASB) published an update to its Accounting Standards in which "fair value accounting" can be used to recognize net income. This move is expected to make it easier for institutions to invest in digital assets.

Finally, after years of speculation, there is a growing sense on Wall Street that the SEC is finally poised to approve a "spot" ETF. What has been so strange about this entire application process is that there is already a much riskier "futures" ETF. That the SEC has dragged its feet on a spot ETF is yet another example of Gensler's strange behavior.

It is perhaps logical for money managers to wonder just what sort of an affect will this spot Bitcoin ETF have on its future price. Currently, there are 2702 active ETFs in the United States, with the AUM under those ETFs being approximately $6.4T.[9] Needless to say, the ETF is the domain of the Vanguards and BlackRocks of the world. That this could lead to market manipulation is not outside the realm of possibility, but I am currently of the belief that having the spot ETF somewhat counters the future's ETF from a leverage standpoint, meaning price volatility could potentially be muted with this ETF approval.

Hashrate

The chart below is a logarithmic depiction of Bitcoin's hashrate (smooth line) along with price action (jagged line) from its creation in 2009 through mid-December of 2023.[10] For speculators, hashrate has never been a major metric, but for those more concerned with Bitcoin as a protocol or a technology, it remains a key indictor, because a growing hashrate implies that the network is getting more secure with time,

---

[9] https://www.statista.com/statistics/350525/number-etfs-usa/

[10] https://www.blockchain.com/explorer/charts/hash-rate

and that the Lindy Effect mentioned previously is likely to eventually apply to Bitcoin.

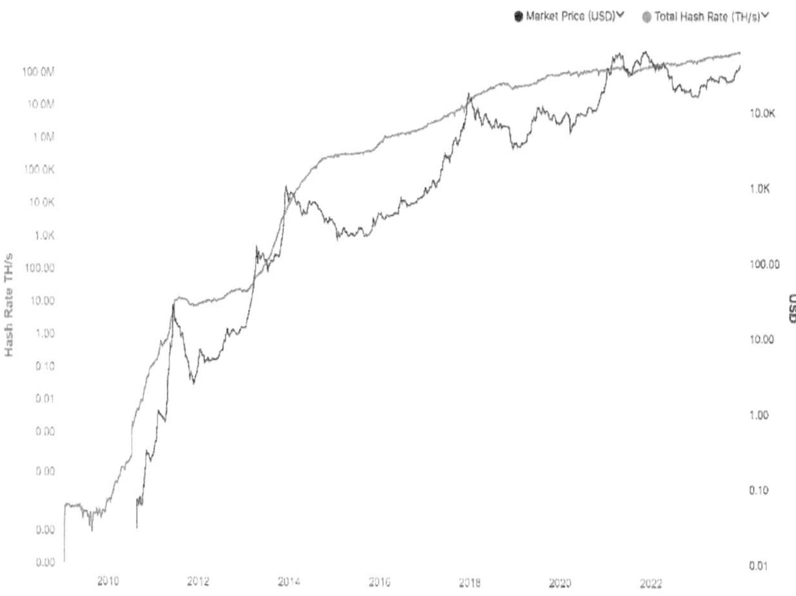

The term "hashrate" is derived from the hash function, which is a mathematical algorithm that miners use to secure transactions and create new blocks. Miners compete to solve complex mathematical problems, and the one who successfully solves the problem gets the right to add a new block to the blockchain and is rewarded with newly created bitcoin and transaction fees. As processing technology has advanced, the manner in which hashrate is measured or depicted has changed as well. As in the chart above, hashrate is today typically depicted as terhahashes per second (TH/s) when the data has been aggregated. Depending on the size of the mining operation, individual miner hashing power can be depicted in hashers per second (H/s) or kilohashes per second (KH/s).

While hashrate is a major component of overall network security, it is not the only metric, as the distribution of miners is also a critical component. This stems from the reality behind a possible "51% attack," whereby one group takes control of the network by owning 51% of the computation power behind the network. Since this is at least theoretically possible, it is worth looking at that major mining distribution across the network currently. The YTD numbers shown below are through mid December of 2023. It should be noted that "Unknown" doesn't mean small and insignificant, it just depicts an aggregation of miners whose operations could not be formally identified.

	Miner / Pool	Percent	Blocks Mined
1	Foundry USA	30.41	16362
2	AntPool	22.71	12219
3	F2Pool	13.433	7227
4	ViaBTC	9.357	5034
5	Binance Pool	8.825	4748
6	Unknown	4.476	2408
7	Mara Pool	3.080	1657
8	Braiins Pool	1.747	940
9	SBI Crypto	1.344	723
10	Poolin	1.292	695
		96.674%	52,013

There are a few items to take from this table. First off, a skeptic might wonder just how possible it is for Foundry

USA to reach 51%, or what sort of growth trajectory it is on. Looking at the data over the course of the past three years, it is ticking upward, having gone from roughly 26.68% in a three-year span to the 30.41 shown on the one year chart. This is not a "non issue," though many in the Bitcoin community contend that the 51% attack is a theoretical concern with no practical possibility.

In addition to the decentralized or distributed mining and hash power, they often make some combination of these additional points:

1. Economic Incentives: Successfully attacking the network would require a massive amount of computational power and resources. If a miner were to invest that heavily in mining equipment, it would make more economic sense for them to use that power to mine honestly and profit from block rewards and transaction fees.

2. Community Consensus: Any attempt to attack the network would likely result in a loss of trust and value in the Bitcoin ecosystem. The community, including developers, users, and businesses, would likely react to defend the integrity of the network, possibly just "forking" the true network and separating from the new, fraudulent network.

3. Self-Regulating Difficulty: The Bitcoin protocol adjusts the difficulty of mining approximately every two weeks to ensure that new blocks are added to the blockchain roughly every 10 minutes. If miners were to suddenly control more than 50% of the hashrate, the protocol would adjust to

increase the difficulty, making it harder for them to maintain control.

Of these three points, the one that I think many Bitcoin advocates gloss over is point number 1. They are correct in their belief that the Bitcoin incentive structure is a major part of why the ecosystem has worked from the very beginning, continues to work today, and is likely to work in the future. The problem with simply thinking in terms of proper incentives though, is that this logic assumes market incentives acted upon by typical, free market participants. Unfortunately, governments don't fall under the category of free market participants. They have the ability to print money, tax residents, buy mining equipment, and to act in ways that would not be economically feasible for any other rational actor.

That governments don't always act rationally is presumably not a point I need to make, but the threat to Bitcoin from a government source isn't likely to come from a minor power, or even a secure major power. Rather, I would contend that the biggest threat is most likely to come from a declining power. Clearly, the United States could be seen as a declining power today, but a declining power still with resources. With a declining population and a shortage of natural resources, China could be deemed a declining power as well, though because of its metoric economic rise, many assume it is too soon to see it on its way down.

While trying to take over the Bitcoin network for economic gain is so improbable as to not merit discussion, gaining control of the network to the point where no one trusts it any longer is not impractical. Elizabeth Warren does not want to take over the Bitcoin network, she wants to end it.

Following China's most recent crypto crack down in June of 2021, there was discernible migration of miner activity from China to the United States. Those like Jason Lowery who see Bitcoin as having potential national security implications certainly saw this as a positive. Rather than seeing this event through the lens of national security, I saw it simply as an example of how point number 3 mentioned above really is the understated key feature of the Bitcoin network.

What most know as the "difficulty adjustment" is a process by which it becomes easier or harder to create and add a new block to the blockchian depending on how much computational power is in the network. The system is intended to ensure that new blocks are created approximately every ten minutes. With Chinese miners shut down, there were fewer computers securing the network and creating new blocks. Despite this, no hacks occurred, blocks kept getting created, and the network kept rolling along. Price action hasn't been a great story for the past two years, but the system itself is running better than ever. Zero hacks. Zero shut downs. Zero countries taking over. Regardless of price action, that's a good story.

7

TAXES

"A fine is a tax for doing something wrong. A tax is a fine for doing something right."

~ *Anonymous*

As much as I would like to gloss over the reality of taxes within this space, Tanya Seda has rightfully encouraged me to dedicate a chapter to this area. Her experience in crypto is ultimately much greater than my own, and so this chapter is truly a collaborative effort that hopefully rounds things out in a way that will further help planners become comfortable within the crypto realm.

While the idea of "crypto friendly" countries has been mentioned previously, it is good to start a tax discussion with some high level, nation state thoughts. As an American, one currently has to view crypto and taxes from a federal and state vantage point almost simultaneously. It is probably not surprising to know that places like Florida and Texas are leaning toward a low or no tax stance on crypto use and trading, while places like New York and New Jersey are going in the opposite direction. Puerto Rico is another location that is currently quite crypto friendly in terms of taxation.

As a financial professional, it is worth knowing that the primary exchanges within the US, both Kraken and Coinbase, do provide meaningful tax compliance tools on their platforms. Retail investors with multiple accounts can struggle to aggregate all of their activity, and so keeping your potential client portfolios in one singular exchange is likely to make the most sense for you.

92

In large part, at the federal level, you can think of crypto derived taxes as falling into two buckets: capital gains and ordinary income. On the ordinary income side of things, there are events like mining based income, staking, hard forks, and airdrops. Besides possibly staking your clients' crypto, this side of taxation isn't likely to concern you greatly. On the other hand, capital gains issues are very much going to need your understanding, as this can include: selling cryptocurrencies, trading one crypto for another, margin trading, and investing in an ICO (Initial Coin Offering).

As capital gains will be the typical concern, the holding time of a digital asset under your management will largely dictate potential tax rates. A cryptocurrency that is bought and sold within one year will incur short term gains at a rate currently between 10 and 37%. Long term rates, a holding of more than a year, fall between 0 and 20% currently. It perhaps goes without saying, but the above rates vary based on overall income for the individual investor.

In January of 2024, as this book was being edited, the SEC approved several Bitcoin "spot" ETFs. This had been expected for some time, and now represents one of the easiest ways for institutional investors to get exposure to Bitcoin. As of this writing, the AUM of the biggest funds:

ETF Name / Ticker	AUM
Grayscale Bitcoin Trust (GBTC)	$28.6 billion
iShares Bitcoin Trust ETF (IBIT)	$2.7 billion

ProShares Bitcoin Strategy ETF (BITO)	$1.8 billion
Bitwise Bitcoin ETF (BITB)	$623.1 million
Invesco Galaxy Bitcoin ETF (BTCO)	$300.0 million
Volatility Shares 2x Bitcoin ETF (BITX)	$222.3 million
ProShares Short Bitcoin ETF (BITI)	$76.6 million

The "spot" ETF approval was strange in the manner in which SEC Chairman Gensler seemed to repeatedly delay the approval of the "risky" asset all the while a "futures" Bitcoin ETF already existed. Regardless, this spot ETF will represent a conventional way for institutional investors to get exposure. From a pure price action standpoint, this may be enough for many of your clients, it will not however equate to your client actually owning Bitcoin. That will be a reality you will need to discuss with them. From a tax perspective, taxes derived from an ETF will fall into the capital gains category.

In addition to the ETF manner of exposure, there are also Bitcoin based IRAs. Some of the most well known are Bitcoin IRA, BitIRA, and iTrustCapital. Like traditional IRAs, there are tax advantages that are probably well understood by you and your clients.

With the above in mind, crypto and taxes is largely about portfolio construction when viewed from the vantage point of financial professionals. This does represent both a challenge and an opportunity. The opportunity lies in the fact that crypto remains volatile. There are large swings in price action. Understanding the cyclic nature of Bitcoin's price action is therefore important.

As of this writing, Bitcoin represents roughly half of the cryptocurrency's $2T market. This is sometimes referred to as the "Bitcoin Dominance." In the crypto space, Bitcoin almost always leads, and then alt coins follow. In the 2023 upward move for crypto, Bitcoin dominance reached as high as about 55%. Historically, traders have taken Bitcoin profits and rolled them into smaller alt coins which have the potential to move higher when conditions are favorable. This is a taxable event that you as a professional money manger must account for. It also restarts the clock in regards to short and long term capital gains.

While the cyclical concept of market dynamics is not new news to you, the cyclical nature of Bitcoin might be. Because new bitcoin is "mined" according to a pre-determined schedule (roughly, every four years), the new supply of bitcoin gets cut in half at a known time. This supply shock, at least for the first decade and a half of Bitcoin's existence has created a four year cycle that seems to almost govern Bitcoin's price action.

Because miners represent how new bitcoin enters the system, and because this constitutes real income on their end, miner sell pressure can be very real going into the "halving" event, as their profit (reward) is about to be cut in half. All of these dynamics matter for you and your client, and you should understand them if you're going to incorporate Bitcoin or crypto into your management services.

Assuming that the majority of your clients are not particularly interested in taking their crypto assets overseas to more crypto friendly jurisdictions (UAE, Malta, etc.) it is worth understanding how Wyoming is becoming to crypto what Delaware is to traditional corporate creation. For example, a flurry of legislative acts, known as the "Blockchain Bills," has made Wyoming a logical place to do business if your business has any crypto or blockchain based components. Three of the most important:

1. HB0070 - This bill, known as the "Digital Assets Act," provides a legal framework for the creation, issuance, and transfer of digital assets on a blockchain. It also allows for the creation of special purpose depository institutions to provide banking services to blockchain companies.

2. HB0185 - This bill establishes a regulatory sandbox for blockchain and financial technology companies to test new products and services in a controlled environment without having to comply with all existing regulations.

3. HB0085 - This bill exempts virtual currency from state property taxation, providing a favorable tax environment for blockchain companies operating in Wyoming.

Quite simply, Wyoming wants to be the crypto capital of the US. This could mean that over time, it is a better place to park assets for your clients. It could represent an aspect of your clients' tax strategy. Because the US regulatory environment is partisan, likely to change, and currently different from state to state, crypto may perhaps represent a new, fundamental way in which you can gain a better understanding of client needs.

Should you be looking to provide crypto related investment services to your clients, some questions worth considering:

1. Is their interest based completely on price action, or does the underlying asset hold value to them, perhaps in the way that some investors want certain tangible assets like gold?

2. Does the interest in crypto represent a long term investment thesis, or is it something based on short term trends?

3. Is portfolio management more about custody or more about actively trading to improve returns?

4. Is crypto to be viewed as a hedge against traditional finance, or perhaps as an easy way to remain liquid while staying in the markets?

5. What professional resources (CPA's, attorneys) do you currently have who have demonstrated some level of crypto expertise?

These are but some of the questions you'll need answers to, and all have tax implications. My involvement with a crypto based hedge fund has proven to me that understanding the tax implications of portfolio management is nearly as important as charting and trading. Exchanges like Coinbase are easy to navigate, and even their institutional or "pro" platforms are easy to maneuver through. This means that trading on highly volatile days can be tempting (up or down), but tax issues might make it pointless.

8

WHAT'S WRONG WITH BITCOIN?

"Nobody can be a great economist who is only an economist - and I am even tempted to add that the economist who is only an economist is likely to become a nuisance if not a positive danger."

~ Frederick A. Hayek

Too Fast, Too Quickly

In the first few days of Donald Trump's second term in office, a flurry of crypto related events took place that seemed poised to usher in a new era in Bitcoin and crypto adoption. From Executive Orders calling for working groups to study the topic, to naming an "AI and Crypto" tzar, to actually announcing plans for a Strategic Bitcoin Reserve, the difference between the Trump Administration and the Biden Administration was not just campaign rhetoric, it was real.

And Bitcoin subsequently fell by 30%.

While I do not consider myself a long time Bitcoin believer, I've been in the space long enough to know that anytime Bitcoin isn't hitting all time highs, the perception is, "what's wrong?" While the short term price gyrations of Bitcoin is not the focus of this book, the dramatic change between the Biden and Trump Administrations is so stark, that this book would be incomplete without addressing this new environment.

Having previously mentioned the Strategic Reserve, that is as good a place to start as any. On the surface, this seems like nothing but good news for Bitcoin holders, and it probably will be. What must be considered though, is most Bitcoin advocates assumed that the United States would be one of the last countries to get on board with Bitcoin. When El Salvador declared it legal tender back in 2021, there were US Senators passing resolutions to condemn the tiny country.

While El Salvador's vocal and official acceptance of Bitcoin was meaningful to some, it was hardly a signal to other nations to begin building their own stockpile. Many assumed that other countries would slowly take an interest, and that over time, the United States would begrudgingly deal with it. All that has now changed with the Strategic Reserve announcement, and that does potentially provide for some degree of risk.

Had adoption been gradual at the nation state level, it is difficult to see there being something like a "currency war" surrounding Bitcoin. That prospect now seems at least possible, though still not probable.

While a Bitcoin style currency war might not be likely, countries can ban its use, as China has done many times. More importantly than its use though, countries could ban the mining of Bitcoin, which China has also done. While the Bitcoin network has never been hacked, the use of quantum computing by a nation state eager to send a competitor back to the stone age is not an impossible scenario. So, in this case, "what is wrong with Bitcoin" may be that it has grown too fast, too quickly. From El Salvador to the United States in four years: even the most adamant supporters must admit to being surprised by this.

Miner Centralization

In addition to the Strategic Reserve, this Administration has also alluded to Bitcoin mining and making the US a hub for this emerging industry. It is certainly no accident that David Sacks has been appointed to serve in a dual capacity, with both AI and crypto policy falling under his purview. The two are certainly linked as they both rely on power and compute in order to be meaningful.

It is here that it must be at admitted that the Trump Administration's belief in Bitcoin could potentially not bode well for future price action. To understand why this could be the case, one need only think through the reality that Bitcoin is truly decentralized. It exists because because nation states have proven over time to not be very good at managing their nation's currency. Should a nation, any nation, push Bitcoin adoption to the point of gaining asymmetric advantage within the network, that could prove problematic.

To be clear, owning a great amount of Bitcoin doesn't give you a greater degree of ownership of the protocol. This is one of the reasons Bitcoin is truly different within the realm of crypto currencies. As a "Proof of Work" protocol, it is the miners, and the nodes within the protocol who guide how the network operates. Even if one were to own 10,500,001 Bitcoin, this would not give that individual a theoretical majority of voting shares within the protocol. If one were to own 51% of the computational power within the network, that would be different, and would not be good for anyone.

Being at the forefront of the Bitcoin mining industry should be a positive for the United States, but ensuring that the mining industry truly remains distributed and decentralized could be a challenge. The desire to "win" vs the desire to encourage other nations to accept this neutral form of money will not be a straight line path, and in many ways, that might represent the biggest challenge facing David Sacks.

The issue of keeping mining truly decentralized and therefore censorship resistant is not something that should be dismissed. In fact, one new mining entity "Ocean" is already sounding the alarm. It's founder, Luke Dashjr, a longtime developer within the Bitcoin protocol, has claimed, "As we stand today, Bitcoin is not a censorship resistant network, rather it just happens to be a network that is not currently being censored. As with other forms of centralization (hardware, firmware, ...), the role of mining pools must change for Bitcoin to exist as a truly decentralized currency."

One of the approaches that Ocean, (not yet large enough to have been listed in the Chapter 6 table), has taken is to give miners within its "pool" much more say in how they mine. What this means at the technical level, is that miners get to design their own templates, meaning they get to control what types of transactions they compete for.

As an example, in the midst of the NFT craze that gripped much of the crypto scene in the previous market upswing, the Bitcoin network was left out of the manic activity because these "Non-Fungible Tokens," or digital trading cards weren't built on Bitcoin. They were largely made, or minted on Ethereum. For most philosophical supporters of Bitcoin, this was a good thing, as they felt that digital representations of dogs, apes, and cats, had no place within the Bitcoin protocol.

In 2023, the idea of Bitcoin "Ordinals" emerged, which was basically an NFT, but on the Bitcoin blockchain. For Bitcoin purists, this was almost scandalous. In a network of truly decentralized miners, there could be some miners who simply do not mine blocks with Ordinals, while others who have no issue with using up blockspace for such activities as digitizing dogs playing poker, will in fact mine new blocks.

While this example hardly explains the entire issue surrounding miner autonomy, it hopefully drives home the point that miners matter more than holders of the coin. There could come a time in which certain miners only mine blocks that will generate large transaction fees. Others might be completely open to Ordinals or whatever activities might be developed in the future. Regardless, the point remains: a US monopoly on Bitcoin mining would not be good for Bitcoin, because what makes Bitcoin special, is that it's as much a protocol as it is money, and the protocol only matters to the extent that it is completely decentralized.

Game Theory

From the inception of Bitcoin, its proponents have often described the idea of some sort of "game theory" as the means by which mass adoption occurs. This concept of game theory typically being referenced is a branch of mathematics that is concerned with competitive situations where choices and actions carried out by one participant depends principally on the choices and actions of the other participants. In the game theoretic of Bitcoin adoption, it has largely been felt that at a certain point, some sort of "mass adoption" would occur because at some point, the masses would realize that everyone else was moving in that direction, so they better get on board.

In this chapter dedicated to "what's wrong with Bitcoin," it is worth exploring what has long been its principal means of marketing: digital gold. On the very day that this chapter is first being written, gold hit an all time high of over $3000 an ounce. Bitcoin on the other hand is struggling to find support at $80,000, down roughly 25% from its all time high. In other words, one asset is flourishing in the uncertain environment of early 2025, while the other is struggling. A skeptic might say that the digital version of gold simply isn't very good in an economic crisis. There could be some truth to that, but in all fairness, the game theoretic of gold has been around for thousands of years.

If it is too soon to assess how Bitcoin handles the turbulence of the Trump Administration, especially in comparison to gold, it is important to point out how game theory most certainly contributed to Bitcoin's upward price action in the month's following its EFT approval. The idea of family offices, accredited investors, and institutional investors "front running" the market saw Bitcoin's price double in 2024. No one wanted to miss the boat, and so many jumped in. Which brings us to a reality that has jolted many Bitcoin advocates: while the Bitcoin ETF made it easy for large investors to get into Bitcoin, it also made it very easy to get out.

With tarrifs, trade wars, and actual wars all making headlines, often times on the weekend, the worst attribute regarding Bitcoin has actually been its liquidity. Weekends have been quite bad for the crypto market since the beginning of Trump's term, and it is not hard to see why. The easiest route to cash for worried investors has often been to unload Bitcoin. At this stage in its life, Bitcoin is perhaps the world's most liquid asset. While that seems like a great attribute, it can be quite bad for price action when news breaks that bombs are falling in Beirut or tariffs are being enforced on Mexico.

In its most pure form, game theory can explain, or perhaps predict outcomes when the participants are all equal. While perfect equality amongst economic participants is never possible, the principal almost demands some degree of equality to be more predictive. Where Bitcoin adoption through the principal of game theory potentially breaks down is when the dominant actor, such as the United States, makes a bold move towards Bitcoin, such as announcing a Strategic Reserve.

Had a country like France, Brazil, or India declared a Bitcoin strategy ahead of the US, there's a chance this could have sent a stronger signal to other nations to follow suit. While the Biden Administration's seizing of Russian assets at the onset of the Ukranian war certainly caused other nations to look the risk of owning US denominated assets, their same risk aversion to American initiatives could extend to Bitcoin if American becomes its chief champion.

To recap, there are three things worth noting that just might be "wrong with Bitcoin" that have come with this new Administration. These are:

1. It's possibly having grown too fast, too quickly.
2. There could be potential problems regarding the centralization of miners
3. Game theory adoption principles having been possibly reversed due to the United States adoption of Bitcoin as a strategic asset.

Of these three concerns, the centralization of miners seems the most likely problem that will have to be addressed, or dealt with. The very creation of the mining pool Ocean confirms that some in the space already see centralization as a problem and are working to fix it.

The idea that Bitcoin has possibly grown too fast, too

quickly, or that the US Strategic Reserve could undo game theory principals could be problematic in the short term. Over time, especially if the United States learns to promote the free market principles that make Bitcoin unique and worth supporting, Bitcoin adoption should only increase.

This chapter, written in the wake of the changes the Trump Administration is clearly bringing, should not be considered "bearish," but rather, just an attempt to identify some potential pitfalls in the midst of all the perceived positive sentiment, perhaps even explaining why the Trump inauguration seems to have created a "local top" for Bitcoin.

In the Conclusion that follows, there is a reference to Central Bank Digital Currencies (CBDCs). As the original version of this was completed, it seemed very likely that this was the direction the Biden Administration was going. Other countries still may, but perhaps the most under reported policy change with the Trump Administration is the Executive Order banning the creation of a national CBDC. While an EO is certainly not law, legislation incorporating the President's wish in this regard is likely to get to his desk. Of all that has been positive for crypto in Trump's first few weeks in office, this shutting down of CBDCs may be the most meaningful.

According to the Experts

The quote that starts this chapter alludes to the the idea that a good economist must ultimately be something of a generalist. Whereas a physicist need not know much about the social sciences to contribute to his chosen field, the discipline of economics is different. The quote was chosen quite purposefully, because after roughly 15 years in existence, there are certainly a lot of financial or economic experts who still do not understand or appreciate it. From J.P. Morgan CEO Jaime Dimon, to Berkshire Hathoway's Warren Buffet, Bitcoin can boast a very long list of naysayers and detractors, most of them specialists who have never actually felt the sting of government induced inflation, perhaps the biggest motivation behind the creation of Bitcoin.

Paul Krugman, a winner of the Nobel Memorial Prize in Economics in 2008 is certainly no fan of Hayek. No doubt, Hayek would have considered him one of those "specialists" who contribute to the "dismal science" moniker given to Economics. Krugman's Nobel prize stemmed from his work in attempting to explain international trade from the vantage point of economies of scale, rather than on geography, climate, or other natural factors.

During the "GFC" or Great Financial Crisis, Krugman was asked what he would do were he running the country. He responded: "capital injection into the financial system, temporary guarantees on interfinancial institution lending to get the crisis under control, a large-scale fiscal stimulus program aiding state and local governments' infrastructure spending to get us out of this recession, and then, after all that, universal health care."[11]

For nearly 25 years, Krugman wrote a twice a week column for the New York Times. With his Nobel prize in hand, he's been a sought after commentator on economic issues for years. His position as an Ivy League

---

[11] https://www.princeton.edu/news/2008/10/13/princetons-paul-krugman-wins-nobel-economics-0

professor has only added to his "expert" status. When he denounces Bitcoin, as he's done regularly, it means something, but what does it really mean?

Ultimately, Krugman's dismissal of Bitcoin isn't because Bitcoin can't work, it's because he doesn't want it to work. Bitcoin simply doesn't fit with his monetary position, a position that espouses extreme money printing in the face of any emergency. Krugman has been bemoaning Trump tariffs as **undoubtedly** inflationary without seeming to acknowledge that extreme money printing has proven to be **demonstratively** inflationary.

Jeff Booth, the Canadian businessman and Bitcoin ambassador mentioned previously, is not an award winning economist. In a recent interview, he made the sober observation: "Bitcoin is just a ledger....you're grappling with something that is imposing a discipline on a world without discipline."

What is wrong with Bitcoin? That's perhaps not the question we should be asking. Rather, we should be contemplating, "what's wrong with us that has made Bitcoin necessary?" The in depth study of Bitcoin is a humbling exercise. My bet is that Krugman's Nobel prize demands he walk proudly upon his firmly held liberal theories, and socialist principals, a place where humility rarely resides. The monetary and fiscal policies he has espoused for years is the reason Bitcoin exists, yet he seems incapable of making the connection. His being a detractor is inevitable, as Bitcoin's very existence, let alone its rapid increase in dollar based value, proves how wrong he has been about so many things.

CONCLUSION

Not long ago, I came across an article that was focused on the downfall of the Soviet Union and how that ultimate downfall stemmed from a collapse in social trust. The author's assertion stemmed from his research that led him to believe that the Red Army by the early 1990's was nearly the only institution that the majority of residents still trusted. They had grown weary of the party, weary of academia, and most certainly weary of government bureaucrats. The one institution that was still held in some measure of esteem was the military.

The Soviet presence in Afghanistan ran from roughly 1979 to 1989. The logic behind that presence was to support the communist government against the insurgent movement most often summarized or thought of as the Mujahideen. Throughout that ten year long engagement the author asserts, the typical Russian was of the belief that the Red Army was winning. Only upon the Red Army's return did the Russian people begin to realize that the war had been lost, and the reality of a decade's worth of fighting for nothing began to truly hit home.

Throughout this short book, I have made references to the power of narratives, myths, or mantras, and so in recognition of that power, I will conclude with another one. Most Americans who remember the formal collapse of the Soviet Union in 1991 also remember the prevailing explanations regarding the collapse. In short, the power and might of the American capitalist system had simply outproduced the Soviets. Our Cold War victory was a victory for capitalism and freedom, while the Soviet's collapse was a clear condemnation of state control and centralized planning.

That the Soviet demise has notable parallels with where America might be treading today seems almost undeniable, but I bring it up not to highlight the pros and cons of centralized economic planning. Rather, I bring it up in order to offer up something that may ultimately be more important: the impact of trust.

The Bitcoin network is sometimes said to be a "trustless" system, and that's not because it doesn't value trust, but because it mathematically facilitates truth. The manner in which it derives consensus, meaning the manner in which everyone on the network comes to agree that the ever growing accounting ledger is correct, is a system upon which almost anything else can be built because trust is at the core.

In an AI world, Bitcoin can almost seem simple, but in an AI world, we are going to need firm foundations upon which to build anything of meaning. In a world in which everything from movies to paintings can be created via Artificial Intelligence, there will be a premium on all those voices, all those concepts, and all those creators who can assert themselves as being fully aware of nuance and context. The Internet made facts cheap, and put a premium on intelligence and creativity. AI is now on the verge of making intelligence and creativity cheap, and so what will it put a premium on? Truth.

While Artificial Intelligence is not the focus of this book, it is part of the story. Over the past year, simply adding "AI" to a company's marketing materials made one an "AI" company. It is so eerily similar to the "dot-com" phenomenon of the late 90's and early 2000's that it would be nearly impossible not to see it. Is Artificial Intelligence eventually going to go into the historical record as just another advancement that ultimately led to higher living standards and higher levels of productivity, or is something different emerging?

The previously mentioned Jeff Booth contends that AI does in fact bring something completely new to the economic equation that has always placed meaningful employment at the top of any government planners wish list. Booth believes that AI will displace employees, and that this displacement will be unlike anything we have ever seen before simply because no other technological advancement has ever come close to being called "intelligent." Because of Booth's belief in a coming wave of structural unemployment, and because he's a believer in the downward price pressure that technology should naturally bring to most every market, he advises the following:

"What if, instead of trying to stop deflation at all costs, we embrace it? ... Deflation becomes something celebrated because it means that we are getting more for less ... We allow ourselves to accept abundance ... As technology removes jobs and fewer overall jobs are needed, prices will keep falling, allowing those who lose jobs a way to share in the benefit of technology abundance without massive transfers of wealth."

Regardless of what you think of Booth's premise, it is at least worth your thinking about the forces at play and the systems upon which those forces operate. A system that demands inflation (our current system) is simply at odds with a technologically advanced system that is by its very nature, deflationary. In other words, these are two forces pulling in the exact opposite direction. Like an evenly matched 4th of July tug-of-war competition, this inflation versus deflation fight will at times appear like a stalemate, with neither side seemingly capable of overcoming the other. But inevitably, one side eventually does win, and the losing side typically ends up falling to the ground, sometimes falling into the water, or sometimes the mud. It's almost always unruly, and oftentimes messy in the end.

That the economic issues that have been mentioned or discussed in this book are profound and difficult would be a gross understatement. From the potential rise of the BRICS nations to the possible demographic collapse of China, we have no shortage of challenges abroad. At home, we are faced with rising debts, and a growing sense that our government has no intention of actually paying back those debts. The impact of a potential US default is a concept few want to contemplate, and one I don't particularly concern myself with in the short term. Rather, I see the United States eventually becoming more like that person who has had too much to drink at the club, and has to ask once the lights come back on, "where did everybody go?"

Whereas the drunk club goer is prone to say things like, "I can still drive," the US government is prone to say things like, "I can still lead." The problem is, neither are likely true and it is this inability to see reality that makes Bitcoin potentially so powerful for you and the clients you serve.

In the very near future, governments are going to roll out Central Bank Digital Currencies, or CBDC's. There will probably be marketing campaigns and PSAs that promote the idea that adopting these CBDC's will make you a patriotic and responsible supporter of cryptocurrencies. That will be a lie. The hallmark of cryptocurrencies is their _decentralized_ nature, and these

CBDC's will be the exact opposite. As a professional manager of other peoples' money, you have a moral and fiduciary obligation to know that.

For me to close this book with price predictions on Bitcoin, Ethereum, or any other cryptocurrency would be a fool's errand. It would imply a level of arrogance that I hope I have not conveyed elsewhere. Understanding this space demands humility, and that will continue to be the case as it evolves. If you are going to begin offering crypto services to your clients, your learning curve will be steep. Interestingly, if you are going to ignore crypto, your learning curve may be even steeper, as you are going to have to explain to clients, based on insight, not ignorance, as to why you are ignoring it. Either way, there is much to learn. Good luck.

ABOUT THE AUTHOR

John considers himself a "traditional technologist," in that he looks at technology as a means to solve perennial problems, not a short term innovation likely to create new ones. As such, John views Bitcoin as a "means" by which we may all have a more abundant "end." Since 2019, he has studied Bitcoin, become a managing partner in a crypto based hedge fund, written numerous articles on the subject, and largely been an advocate for the freedom based principles found within the Bitcoin protocol.